Also by Randy Powell

RUN IF YOU DARE

TRIBUTE TO ANOTHER DEAD ROCK STAR

THE WHISTLING TOILETS

DEAN DUFFY

IS KISSING A GIRL WHO SMOKES
LIKE LICKING AN ASHTRAY?

MY UNDERRATED YEAR

THREE CLAMS
and an
OYSTER

THREE CLAMS
and an
OYSTER

Randy Powell

FARRAR, STRAUS AND GIROUX
NEW YORK

Library of Congress Cataloging-in-Publication Data
Powell, Randy.
  Three clams and an oyster / Randy Powell.— 1st ed.
    p. cm.
  Summary: During their humorous search to find a fourth player for their
flag football team, three high school juniors are forced to examine their
long friendship, their individual flaws, and their inability to try new
experiences.
  ISBN 0-374-37526-7
  [1. Friendship—Fiction. 2. Flag football—Fiction. 3. Humorous
stories.] I. Title.

PZ7.P8778 Th 2002
[Fic]—dc21

                                                    2001054833

To my father, Ray Powell

1

We're throwing the football around on a cool September evening in a small neighborhood park in Seattle, surrounded by trees on three sides, a few blocks from the cemetery.

The three Clams: Rick Beaterson, Dwight Deshutsis, and me, team captain, Flint McCallister.

Our fourth man, our Oyster, Cade Savage, hasn't shown up yet. He's our problem child.

"Anybody see him at school today?" I ask.

"I did." Deshutsis extends his long skinny arms and snags a pass from me over his right shoulder.

"No, you didn't," Beaterson says.

"I didn't say he was *in* school. He showed up after school—in the parking lot."

"Which parking lot?" Beaterson says.

"What difference does that make? The east one."

"What were you doing in the east parking lot?"

"I like parking there sometimes—not very often, but certain times. Is that okay?"

"No. It's weird."

"You saw Savage in the parking lot," I say. "What kind of shape was he in?"

"Define *shape*," Deshutsis says in his clipped professorial tone. "He was sober, I believe. Probably high, although these days he always looks stoned to me. He has that leering grin."

I'm about to throw the ball to Deshutsis, but I hold up when I see him spit a long white strand of saliva into his palms and rub them together.

"Hey!"

"Sorry, sorry."

Beaterson and I have been trying to break him of this new palm-spitting, hand-licking habit he's picked up. He thinks it gives him a better grip on the ball, but it makes the football leather stink of saliva.

Deshutsis squats and wipes his hands on the damp grass, then dries them on the back of his sweats.

"I don't get it," Beaterson says. "Certain times you prefer the east parking lot? What certain times? Certain times of the month? Like when you're having your period?"

"It's called variety," Deshutsis says. "Diversity. You should try it."

A strong wind is blowing from the north. The sky

seems to be getting darker by the minute, although there's still an hour of daylight left.

"Did you talk to him in the parking lot?" I ask.

"There was a big hubbub going on," Deshutsis says. "Bao Alatina was showing off his new Porsche Carrera. There was a crowd of gawkers standing around. Savage drives in—you can hear his car five blocks away—exhaust billowing."

The wind cranks up with another hard gust, bending the trees and sending leaves flying. I toss Deshutsis the football and the wind carries it, but he pulls it in effortlessly.

"Did you talk to him or not?" I say.

Deshutsis gives me a look, tucks the football under his arm, licks his long, narrow fingers, rubs them together, and throws to Beaterson.

"Eventually, yes," he says. "My purpose in talking to him was twofold. First, I wanted to make sure he knew we were having practice tonight, where we were meeting, what time, that sort of thing. Second, I wanted to remind him we're going to the cemetery after the practice. He knew it. He said he'd be here."

"Did you ask him why he skipped school?"

"I didn't have to. He announced it to the whole parking lot. His parents left for Reno this morning for four days."

"I didn't know that," Beaterson says.

"I didn't either," I say.

"He's out of control," Deshutsis says. "I've been saying that for months. You never listen to me. He's getting worse. Somebody—i.e., our team captain—needs to sit him down and straighten him up. He's going overboard on everything—boozing, partying, drugs. He's on self-destruct. He's a time bomb. Just ticking away. Tick tick tick. He's going to explode. Tick tick tick tick."

"Spare us the sound effects," Beaterson says.

"Tick."

"Was that all that happened in the parking lot?" I say.

"No. When I headed for my car, Savage and Alatina had their heads together, deep in conversation. They were planning something, I don't know what. A drug deal, no doubt."

A drug deal. I have to remind myself this is Deshutsis talking. Deshutsis, which rhymes with *he shoots his mouth off*; he shoots us a lot of bull.

"How much longer are we going to wait for him?" Beaterson says.

"What time you got?" I ask.

Beaterson tips his watch, making his forearm and biceps bulge. "Seven-thirty. He's an hour late."

Beaterson's the only one of us who wears a watch. It's a big ugly thing that his older sister, Sari, gave him nine months ago for his sixteenth birthday. He knows it's pretty hideous, but he wears it out of loyalty to his sister. He's very touchy about Sari. She looks a lot like him, short and compact, with thick dark eyebrows, a wide neck, and close-set eyes, which is okay on a guy, but on a girl it's pretty bad luck. Her name is pronounced the same as *sorry*, so over the years some wiseass occasionally says, "Yeah, she's sorry-looking, all right." And Beaterson has made more than one person extremely sorry they said it.

I guess it's time for me to go find a pay phone. None of us, except for Savage, owns a cell phone. We refuse to on principle. I'm not exactly sure what that principle is.

Beaterson and Deshutsis stay behind, in case Savage shows up, while I drive my Ford Escort several blocks in search of a pay phone. When I find one, I call Savage's cell phone. He doesn't answer, so I leave a message. Plunk in more coins, and leave the same message on his home phone. More coins, I call my house and ask my mom if Cade's called, which he hasn't.

I head back to the field, and I am starting to get mad.

This was to be an important night for us. Our flag-football season starts the weekend after this one. We play in a four-on-four league in the eighteen-and-under division. Our team name is Three Clams and an Oyster. This will be our seventh year playing together.

This weekend, we have *five* practice games lined up: one on Friday, two on Saturday, and two on Sunday.

Tonight, Thursday, was to be our night as a team, just the four of us. We'd have a good long practice, go over all our plays and game strategies, get everything sorted out and straightened up. Then we'd go to the cemetery. Of course, it's closed at sundown, so we'd crawl in through the bushes, find the grave of our old friend and original Oyster, Glen Como, and pay homage to him by peeing on his grave.

When I get back to the field, there's still no Savage. Beaterson and Deshutsis have sat down on either end of a bench that faces the street. I sit between them, violating their personal space. The sky has grown a black ceiling. To the northwest, somewhere over Puget Sound, there's a flash of lightning, followed by thunder.

"I am going to strangle him," I say.

"Maybe he's lying in some ditch," Beaterson says.

"More like lying on some bitch," Deshutsis says.

Beaterson looks at him. "Not bad. You just think that up?"

"His behavior has been deteriorating for months," Deshutsis says. "Ever since Glen died. He's a time bomb. But does anyone ever listen to me?"

"If you say 'tick tick' I'm going to smack you," Beaterson says.

Long minutes pass.

There's a rumble of thunder. It sounds like an avalanche of boulders.

We sit like three geezers at the barber shop waiting for a haircut.

"We should have gotten a fifth man," I say. "We kept putting it off. It's my own fault. Practically every other team has a five-man roster, but here we are with only four."

"The Doctor Lauras only have a four-man roster," Deshutsis says.

"Yeah, and they've had to forfeit some games when one of their guys was sick," I say.

A car goes by. It's not Savage's.

"How much longer you want to sit here?" Beaterson says.

"What time is it?"

"Five to eight."

"Pleasant evening, though," Deshutsis says. "A lot of activity in the substratosphere. You got your cumulus. You got your leaves swirling around. You got thunder and lightning to the north, but it's a cloudless sky to the south. There's a storm coming. Big one. Going to be a real blow overnight."

"Cumulus," Beaterson mutters, shaking his head. "There's not going to be any storm. They said it's going to be a mild, starry night."

"They. You mean the meteorologists? They don't know anything."

"And you do."

"It's going to be a big one."

"You don't get big storms in September," Beaterson says. "They don't come until October."

"This one's coming from the north. It's the Nanook squall."

"Shut up," Beaterson says. "Nanook squall."

We watch the trees bend and shake in the wind.

"What I don't understand is," Beaterson says, "you saw Savage in the parking lot three hours before we were supposed to meet here. You talked to him. You claim he said he was coming. Yet you give us some stupid story about him and Alatina making plans and cooking something up. Is that what you want us to believe?"

"Oh, okay, yeah, I made it all up. You got me. I made it up about the storm tonight, too. It's all a lie. And Yom Kippur, there's no such thing. I invented that, too."

"Shut up," Beaterson says. "God!"

A woman jogger in a runner's bra with a frustrated dog on a short leash comes by on the sidewalk. The woman's bare back and shoulders are red and sweaty.

Beaterson calls out in his deep, resonant voice: "Yow! You have a beautiful body."

The woman cuts us a glance as she jogs past.

"I made her day," Beaterson says.

More cars go by.

"Maybe we should go to the cemetery tonight anyway," Deshutsis says.

"Not without Savage," I say.

Our ritual demands that we go there as a team, a unit.

"Let's call it a night," I say. "He'll probably get ahold of me eventually, but if he doesn't, you guys can grab him at school tomorrow."

Beaterson and Deshutsis both know I'm excused from going to school tomorrow, because I'm getting up at five-thirty to drive my folks up to Vancouver, B.C., to drop them off at the cruise ship that's taking them on a five-day Alaskan cruise. Since I'm an only child, I'll be on my own for the next five nights.

"I can't wait to hear what his excuse is," Deshutsis says.

There's another sheet of lightning to the north, followed by a loud boom and a blast of wind in the trees.

"Heap big storm coming," Deshutsis says. "Nanook squall. Bad omen. Baaaad omen."

"Will you please shut up," Beaterson says.

"Tick tick tick," says Deshutsis.

2

"*Flint . . .*"

A voice from way off. The east parking lot, maybe. Coming from inside a cloud of black smoke from a lime-green '91 Camaro.

"Flint . . ."

I try to open my eyes, but they're glued shut.

"Flint . . ."

It's my dad. He's tugging at my arm. I protest. It can't be five-thirty . . .

"Flint!"

I open my eyes. Dad doesn't look too awake, either. I check my clock radio. It's 1:14.

"Whuh."

Dad's holding the cordless phone out to me. "It's for you."

"Huh?"

"It's Cade Savage. He says he's in a jam. I want you to remind him that it's one-fifteen in the morning on a school night and I don't care what kind of jam he's in. If it's that big a jam, he can call nine-one-one. You have to drive us to the boat in four hours."

Dad lays the phone on my chest. When I pick it up and listen, I hear mouth-breathing.

"Cade?"

"Flint. Hey. How's it going?"

I groan.

"Hey, I was wondering if you could do me a favor."

As I raise myself into a sitting position, I listen to Cade describe his predicament. His voice is slower than usual, slightly hoarse. I can't tell if he's been drinking, or if he's coming down from a pot high, or if he's just tired. He says his car is in a creek bed. He's got a passenger with him. If he doesn't get the passenger home very soon, the passenger's father is going to do a Jack the Ripper on his testicles.

"Who's the passenger?" I say.

"Does it matter?"

My dad is frowning. I sit up another notch. In my phone ear, Cade is telling me his location. In my other ear, Dad is asking me if Cade's been drinking.

"Have you been drinking?" I say into the phone.

"Who, me?"

I look at my dad and shake my head. My mom enters the room as Cade continues his incoherent directions. The ravine, the winding road down to the bottom, the deserted little turnaround at the end of a dead-end road. Fortunately, I know where he's talking about, not that I've ever used it for the purpose Cade and his passenger were evidently using it for tonight.

I hang up and roll out of bed.

"Is he all right?" Mom asks.

"Yeah."

"I don't suppose he has towing insurance," she says.

"He's got a cable in his trunk, Mom. That's as close to towing insurance as he's ever going to get."

I hunt around my room for my clothes.

"I don't think you should go out there," Mom says. "It's the middle of the night. There's a storm. Bryce?"

"We're leaving for Vancouver in four hours," Dad says. "This is no time to be playing Auto Angel."

"Trees are toppling over out there," Mom says.

"The roads are slick," Dad says.

After I get my clothes on, I head downstairs. Mom and Dad follow me.

"He shouldn't have been out driving this time of night," Dad says. "Can't he call his parents?"

I look at my dad. "He's got a passenger. This wouldn't be a good one to bring the parents in on."

"Oh."

"Besides, they're in Reno."

I put on some old tennis shoes—ones I won't mind

getting muddy—and splash cold water on my face from the kitchen faucet.

Mom and Dad watch.

"You awake?" Dad says.

"Yeah."

"You sure?"

"Yeah."

"You want me to make you some coffee or something?"

"No."

"Take the Explorer," he says.

"Thanks."

"You put a dent in it, I'll . . ."

"Just be careful," Mom says. "Please."

There's almost no traffic on the roads. The wind howls, then lulls, then howls again, but it's stopped raining and the pavement is drying quickly. I maneuver around tree branches and marauding garbage cans. It's scary and exhilarating at the same time.

FM radio is crystal clear.

It takes me a half hour to drive to the road that winds its way down to the bottom of the ravine. When the road bottoms out, you can either keep going straight and continue up the other side and out of the ravine or take a right, down a side road. I take the right. The yellow sign that says NO OUTLET has been plowed over by a car and is leaning against a tree. There are a few houses set way back, and the creek parallels the road. It's about as dark as you can get. The road eventually dead-ends in a gravel turnaround. Beyond that is a shrubby incline leading down to the creek bed. My headlights shine on Cade's Camaro, its front end pointing at me at a weird angle.

Cade and his passenger shield their eyes from my beams. I get out and stand in front of the headlights and wave, to let them know it's me, in case there can be any doubt.

Cade scrambles up to meet me.

"How'd you manage that?" I say above the wind.

Cade's long blond hair is blowing wildly. He's wearing a short-sleeved shirt that shows off his muscles. I'm five-eleven, and Cade Savage is about four-six, including his hair. His nose comes up to my belly button. He's all muscle—he's built like a weight lifter. He's not really a dwarf, although his legs are shorter than they should be and slightly bowed. His head and torso are normal-sized—that is, they'd fit perfectly on a guy who's a foot taller. An indisputably handsome guy (he'd be the last one to dispute it), Cade's got that blond hair, a tanned spotless complexion, and eyes that are the same color as some shallow lagoon in Tahiti.

He explains that he and the girl (whom I still can't identify) were parked in the turnaround, making out.

Somebody's knee or elbow popped the floor shifter into neutral. The parking brake on that rust heap has always been burned out, and before Cade could straighten up and stomp on the brake pedal, the car rolled backward, over the edge, down the incline, and into the creek bed.

"Who is she?" I ask.

He hesitates. "Kat Olney."

"You that desperate?"

He grins, the corners of his mouth turned down, making him look pathetic.

I shake my head. "I should leave you in the swamp."

He keeps grinning.

He's already hooked one end of the cable to his front axle, so after I back the Explorer as close to the edge as I can, Cade attaches the other end of the cable to the Explorer's trailer hitch. He tells Kat to get behind the wheel to steer, while he shoves and rocks his Camaro from behind. Meanwhile, gunning the Explorer in low, hoping to hell I don't fry the transmission, I slowly pull the Camaro out of the creek bed and up the slope. Cade whoops and raises his arms in victory. I get out and give Kat a thumbs-up, but she just sits there looking totally pissed off, as usual.

Cade is loving this.

After making sure his car will start, he comes over to me and shakes my hand. "I owe ya, big guy," he says. "I'm gonna scoot the lady on home. How about letting me buy you some breakfast at The Coffee Spot? You don't want to go back to your nice warm bed."

I do, but I also want to strangle him. Besides, I can snooze on the way up to Vancouver.

So I follow the Camaro to Kat's house, over in Ridgefield. Kat gets out and stomps up her driveway. No good-night nookies for Cade. I have a feeling this is their first and last date.

Ten minutes later, when we get to The Coffee Spot, Cade goes to the rest room to wash up while I use his cell phone to call my dad and let him know everything's okay. I decide not to strangle Cade until he's bought me breakfast.

3

"*Uh-oh.*" Cade peers into his wallet.

We're sitting in a booth in the nonsmoking section. In the next booth, four city light guys, who've obviously been working overtime in this storm, are eating and talking loudly.

"Man, all I have left is two bucks," says Cade. "I started out tonight with two twenties. I can't believe I spent thirty-eight bucks on Kat Olney." He looks up from his wallet and registers my glare. "What?"

"You stood us up."

"Oh. Yeah." He bows his head for a moment. Then he leans forward and glances left and right and licks his lips, which is usually a sign that he's about to tell a dirty joke or brag. "Listen, I'm only human. The temptation was too much. She comes flouncing up to me in the east parking lot and wants to know if I—"

"I don't want to hear about it," I say. "We sat around

waiting for you for two hours. You didn't even call me and leave a message."

"What are you, my old lady?"

I start to go for his throat, but an elderly waitress waddles over with her pad and pen.

"Everything okay, boys?"

"Could be worse," Cade says, flashing her his smile.

"Looks like you got dirty, sweetie. You get blown over by the wind out there?"

"Fell in a swamp," Cade says. "Right where I belong."

"Oh, now, don't say that about yourself."

After she takes our breakfast orders (which I'm going to have to pay for), Cade grins at me and says, "You'd better relax and quit staring at me like that. People're going to think we're a couple of fags having a lovers' spat."

"You screwed us last night," I say. "That's a bad way to start the weekend, a bad way to start the season. It's bad luck."

"Sorry. No excuse. I got sidetracked."

"You want to be on our team or not?"

"What do you mean? Of course I do. Don't rag on me, Flint."

"We have to be able to count on you."

"We can—you can."

"We don't have a fifth guy. One of us doesn't show up, we're out of luck."

"I know that."

"You know we've got a practice game tonight, at Interbay. Marty's Texaco, six o'clock."

"Right."

"I want you there at five. Not five-thirty or five-ten. Five o'clock."

"Don't talk to me like I'm a retard, Flint."

"You do something like that to us again, I'll . . ."

"You'll what?"

"I'll think of something. For starters, I'll tell Beaterson and Deshutsis about tonight. Every single detail. Including Kat Olney."

Cade's grin wilts. "Come on."

"I mean it."

"You wouldn't do that to me."

"You screw us again, I promise I will."

"Don't blackmail me."

"You better decide whether you want to be on our team or not."

"I do. I am. Quit raggin' on me. If I wanted a wife, I'd get married. I wouldn't do that to you, threaten you like that. You tell them about Olney, they'll never let me hear the end of it. They needle me enough as it is. That's why I called *you*, not Beaterson or Deshutsis. You're the one I trust. You wanna hit me, go ahead. But don't be, like, *mean* about it."

I sink back into the booth. The waitress comes with

our orange juice. I take a long drink, and try to calm down.

I guess I do sound like an old nag.

I want to go home and crawl back into bed—even if it's only for an hour.

Being home alone for the next five nights is going to be strange.

After a while, the waitress brings our food. I survey my hashbrowns, sausage links, eggs, and whole wheat toast, then look across the table at Cade. The edge of the table comes up to his chest. He could actually benefit from using a child's booster seat. I love the guy, but he's so pathetic sometimes.

The city light crew in the next booth are laughing about something.

"I didn't know your folks went to Reno," I say.

"Pretty spur-of-the-moment," he says. "They left this morning. I offered to drive them to the airport, but my dad says, hell no, he'd rather shell out fifteen bucks a day in parking, just to keep me from getting my hands on his new truck."

"You skipped school?"

"I needed to catch up on my sleep. Your folks are going on a cruise, aren't they?"

"Yeah, today."

"How do you like that, we're both emancipated. I

feel like doing some kick-ass partying. You know what my new philosophy is? I'm going to be a hedonist. A guy who lives for fun. A guy who's willing to do anything in the name of his own pleasure. Grab it today, 'cause tomorrow might never come."

"You're off to a great start," I say. "Going out with Kat Olney and driving into a creek bed."

"You gonna keep bringing that up on me?"

"That's the downside of hedonism."

Cade shoves a big slab of French toast into his mouth.

"What's with you and Alatina?" I ask.

"Oh, so Deshutsis couldn't wait to tell you about that, huh?"

"Yeah, he could wait. Two hours of sitting on our butts waiting for you."

"You know what your trouble is, Flint? You're stodgy. You and Beaterson and Deshutsis, you spend too much time in your little closed-in world. Everything's such a big deal, everything's crisis time. You guys need to kick back, break your old habits. Get out of your rut. You're so set in your ways. You're like, 'Oh, no, this was the night we were supposed to *practice* and go to the *cemetery*. Oh, no, we didn't do it. Oh, heavens.' Man, ease up."

It's funny, I've always thought my problem is that I'm not intense enough, rather than being too intense.

Maybe that's because I spend so much time with Beaterson and Deshutsis. Compared to those two, I'm ultra laidback.

"You need to ease up, too," I say. "On the booze and chemicals and partying."

"Hark, do I hear Deshutsis talking?"

"We're all worried about you. You need to get control of yourself."

"Why?"

"Because we need you on our team."

"Oh, I appreciate that." He nods and looks away. So help me, I can't tell whether he's sincere, sarcastic, embarrassed, or what. He's still nodding, and his mouth has that little smirk with the corners turned down.

"How you doing, anyway?" I say.

"Don't worry," he says. "I got it under control."

Other than football practices, I really haven't seen much of Cade. During the summer, he worked at North City Auto Parts, doing deliveries, while I worked full-time in a luggage-company warehouse. Cade also had to go to summer school to make up credits, because he got in all kinds of trouble last year and ended up getting suspended. Dumb pranks, mostly, the kind of stuff people do when they're drunk. Things like sticking a guy's trumpet in the toilet, setting off firecrackers, racing his Camaro on the athletic fields.

His grandma died last winter and left his parents

some money. His dad bought a truck and a boat, and let Cade use the boat a few times, and Cade took me, Beaterson, and Deshutsis waterskiing on Lake Washington. But Cade wanted to go a lot more than we wanted to. We preferred to spend most of our free time playing pickup basketball, softball, and flag football. So Cade found other people to take waterskiing.

I notice he's chuckling about something.

"What?" I say.

"I was just remembering something," he says. "Remember that time we all stayed overnight at Glen's? We camped out in his backyard in his tent?"

"Yeah. Five of us in one tent."

"We had a junk-food extravaganza," Cade says. "Middle of the night, Glen wakes up, 'Ohh, I gotta puke, ohh, lemme out.' Naturally, he's farthest from the tent flap. So he's like crawling over us in our sleeping bags. He finally makes it to the flap, sticks his head out, and just starts barfing his guts out and ripping these big old farts, so he's got it coming out both ends at the same time, and we're trapped in there, we can't escape."

Cade puts his hands over his face, he's laughing so hard. The city light guys stop talking and look over at him, because it's hard to tell whether he's laughing or sobbing.

Cade has told me that he still hears a sound, so loud and clear it wakes him up at night. *Plock*, he says—the hard, sharp sound of a bowling ball hitting a single pin. It's the sound of Glen Como's head hitting the rock and splitting open. Not a soft or squishy sound, not like a pumpkin, but the sound of bone on rock. And Glen's breath going out of him in a slow groan, *huuuuuuh*. The last noise Glen Como ever made. Cade's face was inches away, watching him die. *One eye staring at me, the other rolling up into his head somewhere and showing nothing but white, all milky and white, no eyeball at all, just the white.*

That's what Cade remembers, more than the blood.

A little more than two years ago, the summer before ninth grade, Cade went camping with Glen Como and his family. The two of them were fooling around on a bridge, ten feet above a dried-up creek bed. They were just shoving each other, goofing around, and somehow they both went over, and Cade landed on top of Glen Como, and Glen Como's head hit a rock the size of a football.

When Cade's finished laughing, we sit quietly in the booth for a while. Cade sticks his napkin in his ice water and watches the napkin absorb the water.

"Yeah," he says. "That night was the hardest I've ever laughed in my life." He smiles and nods his head slowly. "I'm okay. Five o'clock. Interbay field. I'll be there, Cap'n, don't you worry."

4

It's after five the next day when I pull into the parking lot of Interbay field.

Branches from last night's storm litter the lot, but this evening is calm, and there are patches of blue in what's left of the daylight. The air smells and feels like fall.

Twelve hours ago I drove my folks up to B.C.—or rather, I snoozed while my dad drove—wished them a good cruise, assured them I'd be fine, promised my mom I'd clean the house, promised my dad I'd leave the Explorer parked in the garage, turned around and drove home, cleaned the house, ate leftover Chinese food, napped for two hours, woke up a half hour ago, grabbed a can of Coke, and drove over here in my Escort.

Beaterson and Deshutsis are already here, having driven over together in Beaterson's car.

We're wearing our clamshell-colored Three Clams and an Oyster team jerseys and our football cleats.

There's no sign of Cade or his Camaro.

"Any word from him? You see him today?"

They shake their heads. They tried calling him throughout the day, but never got ahold of him.

"When I talked to him last night, he promised he'd be here," I say.

"What was his excuse?" Deshutsis says.

I shake my head. "He just said he got sidetracked."

Deshutsis looks at me. "That's all?"

I shrug. "It was late when he called me back. I was asleep."

We start tossing the football around, like yesterday, only I have them run some patterns so I can air out my arm. I glance over at the parking lot every minute or so.

Pretty soon, the guys from Marty's Texaco arrive in two separate cars. Lyle Gomez, the team captain, and his four teammates greet us, and we all shake hands. They set up camp about twenty yards from us, getting out the orange cones they've brought to mark the sidelines and end zones, and start going into their pregame stretching and warm-ups.

Marty's Texaco won the division last year, and they probably have one of the best teams in the league, so we're lucky to get a chance to test ourselves against them in this practice game. I think we've improved, and this game should give us a good idea of how competitive we'll be this season.

Besides regular season play, there are four-man flag-football tournaments held year-round, all over the region. The first big one is next month down in Astoria, Oregon, and there's another one after that in Boise. We plan to enter as many as we can, even more than last year. That means having to stay overnight in a motel room, which isn't too expensive when you can split the cost four ways—plus meals and gas.

Before Glen died, we relied on his dad for transportation. That guy was our biggest fan; he loved watching us play, and he'd shoot the whole game on video so we could study it. He came to just about every regular season game, and he even enjoyed taking us to out-of-town tournaments.

After Glen died and we started ninth grade, we had to scramble to find transportation. This is really the first full season that we have our own cars.

One of these days, we hope to get a sponsor who will help finance our travel expenses. That's really been on our minds a lot the past year. There's a store in Seattle called Rain City Athletic Apparel that has been looking for a team to sponsor; but in order for us to have any hope of getting them as a sponsor, we've got to start out the first half of the season with a decent record, we have to be reliable and good models and all that, and we have to do well in a couple of early tournaments. Then, if we keep on knocking on their door, they might just pick us up midway through the fall season and start paying our

way to tournaments all over the western United States—
and that would include spring and part of summer as
well. Naturally, we'd have to change our name to Rain
City Athletic Apparel.

"So, Flint," Lyle says, walking over to me from his camp,
"you seem to be a man short."

"Yeah. Cade Savage. He's on his way."

Lyle nods and spits. A couple of his players are setting up the orange cones to mark the sidelines, end zones,
and first-down lines.

A four-man flag-football field is eighty yards long
by about forty yards wide. It is divided into four lines,
twenty yards apart. Those are the first-down lines. In con-
ventional football, you have to go ten yards to get a first
down; in flag football, you just have to cross the nearest
line to get a first down.

Lyle looks at his watch and clears his throat. "It's
past six. We're ready to roll."

I nod stupidly. What can I say? I keep looking toward the parking lot. Everybody's just standing around or
idly tossing a football.

Lyle spits and checks his watch again. He goes over
to his equipment bag and returns with a cell phone,
which he hands to me without having to say why.

I start calling the same numbers, in the same order,

that I called last night. "Cade," I say to his two sets of voice mail, trying not to sound hysterical, "we're here at Interbay. Everybody's waiting for you." I give him Lyle's cell-phone number and tell him to call and let us know where he is. Lyle looks away from me out of courtesy, or pity. I check my answering machine at home. I get out my address book that has the names and phone numbers of all the other team captains and everybody I know. I call North City Auto Parts, but Cade's boss says he wasn't scheduled to work today. I consider calling Alatina, even Kat Olney, but I don't have their numbers.

"He'll call," I say, handing Lyle back his phone. "Maybe we could play three-on-four till he gets here."

Lyle nods slowly and spits again. His teammates are grumbling. They came here for a serious practice game, four-on-four, not some half-assed pickup game.

I go over to where Beaterson and Deshutsis are standing and put my address book back in the equipment bag.

"Fantastic," Deshutsis says. "Just fantastic."

Ten minutes pass. Lyle's cell phone doesn't ring. I glance over at Lyle and see him talking on somebody else's cell phone. Pretty soon he comes trotting over to us. At the same instant, a couple of his teammates jog out to the field and start collecting the orange cones.

"Flint," he says. "Sorry. We're checking out. I called

the captain of Cow's Muzak. They're up at Harman Park looking for a game. We're going to head up there and play them. No offense."

"No, that's okay," I say. "Sorry we wasted your time, Lyle."

"Yeah, too bad, we were looking forward to playing you guys. Now we'll just have to wait till the season starts. Hey, you know, as a team captain, Flint, I recommend you get one of these." He holds up his phone. "They really come in handy in screwups like this. Another thing—I know it's none of my business, but why in the heck do you guys only have four men on your team? If you had gotten a fifth guy . . ."

"I know, I know. You're right, there's no excuse."

Beaterson, Deshutsis, and I sit down on a nearby bench and watch Lyle and his gang climb back into their two cars and drive away.

We sit looking out at the lighted field. Fog and mist are rolling in from Puget Sound.

"Well," Beaterson says. "Here we are again."

"How can he do this to us?" I say. "I talked to him last night."

"I say he's history," Deshutsis says. "We dish him. Dump him."

"I guess we'd better go back to your place and re-group," I say to Deshutsis. "Figure out what our options are. I don't know. Maybe he's hurt somewhere."

"Shee!" Deshutsis says. "He's gone haywire, that's his only excuse. Face it. What he's doing is forcing us to take a good hard look at reality. And the reality is . . ." Deshutsis raises his index finger, then withdraws it.

"What's the reality?" Beaterson says.

"I'll let you know when I figure it out."

A green car pulls into the parking lot. For a moment, I perk up, thinking it could be a Camaro. Four guys get out. They look about our age. They're wearing sweats and heading over to this empty field. Kicking a soccer ball. Soccer players. Lousy soccer players.

"Let's get out of here," I say.

5

Back at Deshutsis's apartment, we're eating left-over pizza from his refrigerator. I've spent the past half hour with my address book and the telephone, trying to track Cade Savage down, leaving messages all over the place. There's no trace of him.

We have the apartment to ourselves. Deshutsis's older brother, Bob, is out with his girlfriend.

Deshutsis's parents are in Ontario watching the Canadian Open golf tournament. They are golf groupies, which means they spend most of the year traveling from city to city, following the PGA tour. They've raised three successful daughters and a successful son, Bob, who was a top-notch high school golfer and graduated two years ago. Now he's studying major-appliance technology at a nearby voc-tech college.

Their fifth child, Dwight, is the only one they haven't yet raised successfully, but they've run out of gas.

Up until a year ago, the entire Deshutsis clan lived in a huge house on a gigantic lot with a creek running through it, a circular driveway, elm trees, a tree house, a rope swing, raccoons, and a German shepherd named Rowdy. When Deshutsis's parents reached retirement age, which happened to be the same time they petered out being parents, they sold the property to a developer for a fortune and retired.

So Dwight had to say good-bye to the raccoons and trees and rope swing, and his parents rented him and Bob a three-bedroom apartment in this big, beautiful complex. His parents live in the guest room when they're in town.

None of the Deshutsises will ever have to worry about money.

As for Rowdy, he was sent to live on a friend's farm and is very happy (so Dwight has been told by his parents and chooses to believe; Beaterson and I have our suspicions).

"You figure it out yet?" Beaterson says to Deshutsis.

"Figure what out?"

"The reality. What the reality is that we have to face."

Deshutsis looks down and frowns. "Yes. We're wasting our time."

"If you mean sitting in this apartment eating pizza

when we should be playing flag football, I'd agree with you," Beaterson says.

Deshutsis takes a bite of his pizza. "The reality is, Savage has made his choice and now he has to face the consequences." For some reason, when he finishes this statement, he purses his lips and kisses the back of his hand.

"Unless he's cracked up in some ditch somewhere," I say.

"Nah, he's goofing off, all right," Beaterson says. "He's thumping his nose at us."

"Which is considerably noisier and more painful than thumbing it," Deshutsis says snidely.

I walk over to the sliding window that leads to the balcony. The apartment overlooks a courtyard, which contains an enclosed heated swimming pool and a Jacuzzi. Both are unoccupied right now, glowing, very inviting. There's a cabana farther up by the main entrance.

"What are the chances," I ask, looking out the window, "of Savage having a good reason for not showing up and not calling?"

Nobody answers.

Up until the summer Glen died, we did have a five-man roster. Glen was actually the founder of our flag-football team, and he was the one who dubbed us Three Clams and an Oyster. That was in fifth grade, in the eleven-and-unders.

All five of us absolutely hated soccer, which dominates all the Seattle parks and recreation centers in the fall. "Real" football—eleven-man contact with pads and helmets—is so politically incorrect in our area that it's practically nonexistent until high school. Yet we loved football, so it was Glen Como and his dad who led us to the Pacific Northwest Flag Football Club, and to organized four-man flag football. We became addicted to it.

I was the quarterback, because I had the arm. Glen said I should be the captain, too, because he thought the quarterback and captain should always be the same person, and we did whatever Glen said. Glen always called the shots, always made the decisions.

Glen was the Oyster.

"How come you're the Oyster?" we asked him more than once.

He was a soft, pudgy, slow-footed guy. His face was covered with freckles. He had a very pronounced widow's peak on his forehead, and a quiet, confident way. "I'm the Oyster because I hike the ball. That's why."

We didn't get it.

"The Oyster is the hiker," he said. "The delivery system."

We still didn't get it.

"You guys," he said, pointing at me, Beaterson, and

Deshutsis, "are the talent. The Clams. Cade, you are the alternate, the reserve. And me, I'm the weak link, the odd man out, but I got the pearls."

We still didn't get it, but we gave up asking for clarification. We were the Clams, he was the Oyster, fine with us.

Cade loved his role of just being the alternate, the backup, who spent 90 percent of the game watching and cheering from the sidelines, and coming in on the odd play when somebody, usually Glen, needed a rest. I think Cade was happy just being one of us, without actually having to get out there and play.

When Glen Como died, Cade had to step in as the full-time Oyster.

We've talked about adding a fifth guy, and we've even tried out a few, but nobody seems right.

Adding a fifth man is sort of like adopting a new brother. Or maybe like bringing on a new musician to your band: the guy not only has to be talented but has to love the same music and be on the same wavelength. And it's been hard finding somebody like that, given our wavelength. If we find somebody we like, he's not good enough; if he's good enough, he gets on our nerves or just doesn't quite fit as a friend.

Besides, it just seemed too weird adding a guy after Glen died. Glen Como was one of a kind.

So, what to do?

We decide to call Jeff Skattem the regional director of the flag-football club, pray he's still there on a Friday night, and ask him if it's possible, at this late date, to add a fifth guy to our roster.

And if he says yes?

Find a fifth guy.

Miraculously, Jeff answers the phone. As I explain the situation, I picture him sitting at his messy desk, listening intently. When I finish, there's a short pause. Too short.

"Sorry, Flint. It's too late, past the deadline. You had right up until last Wednesday to add a name to your roster. But that's why we have a deadline. It wouldn't be fair to the other teams if we made exceptions."

"I understand." I hesitate, and take a deep breath. "Okay, how about instead of adding a fifth guy, we dump a guy and bring in someone to replace him?"

This time, the pause is longer. I hear Jeff breathing.

"You really feel like you have to do that?"

"Cade Savage has gone AWOL. He's deserted us."

"You're not just dumping him because you've found somebody better. Be honest with me, Flint."

"No. I swear to God. We don't even have anybody yet. We're going to have to scramble to find somebody to take his place. We don't want to dump him at all. It's almost like he's the one who's dumped us."

"Well . . ." Jeff's thinking again. "Technically, it's still a violation, because you're not supposed to change your roster after the deadline, and you're still adding a guy—although, in this case, you're also dropping a guy. I don't think any of the other teams will squawk too much."

I look at Beaterson and Deshutsis, and nod.

"You're going to have to hustle, though, Flint," Jeff says. "I'm putting the schedules together this weekend. You're going to have to find your replacement, have him fill out all the eligibility forms, have his parent sign the insurance waiver and consent forms, and you're going to have to bring me all that paperwork—to my house. I'm sending the schedule and team rosters to the printer's Sunday night, so I can get them back in time to distribute at the captains' meeting next week. So you have until Sunday, day after tomorrow, let's say five o'clock, no later. You think you can get it to me by then?"

"We'll do it, Jeff. Guaranteed."

6

For the next half hour, we discuss possible candidates. The problem we're up against is that a lot of the decent athletes are already tied up playing real football or soccer, or running cross-country, or working a part-time job. Or they're just not committed. Or not compatible with us.

Realistically, there are only two possible choices.

The first is Rachel Summerfield.

She's a girl, which of course would be a bit of an adjustment for us. There are a few girls who play on other teams, so it wouldn't be a problem with the league or anything. But we don't really know her that well. She doesn't even go to our high school. We only know her from playing against her in pickup basketball at the community center. That, plus seeing her skiing a few times—she's a hotdogger on the ski slopes. We've never actually played flag football with her.

So, why are we even considering her? Because she

happens to be one of the best and purest athletes we've ever seen.

For the past year or so, whenever I run into her, she always says she'd be interested in joining our team if we ever needed an extra person. She's not shy about asking, and she really does seem interested, which kind of massages our egos.

"How about it?" I say. "Should I give her a call, see if she's available for a tryout?"

"I say go for it," Beaterson says.

But Deshutsis is shaking his head.

"Why not?" Beaterson and I say.

"Because she's a female. A not-bad-looking female. That will cause too many complications and awkward situations. A certain great philosopher once said, 'Girls are girls, and boys are boys, and mixing them in nondating situations only causes complications.' In other words, don't ever try to make a girl one of the guys. It's too much of a distraction. Lust is one of the major distractions of life. It's one thing to play basketball against her. It's quite another to have her on our team."

There's a moment of silence, as Beaterson and I let this sink in.

Deshutsis continues. "We wouldn't act the same around a girl as we would a guy. We wouldn't be as relaxed. Wouldn't be as much *ourselves*. We might try to show off more. She'd cramp our style. Inhibit us. Our

freedom to fart and burp, or chase after women. We'd always be conscious of this female presence."

Okay, we decide to hold off calling Summerfield.

The other prospect is a guy in our class, Thor Hupf. Thor
is tall, rangy, quick, and very well coordinated. He's also a
super-nice guy, and brainy without being a show-off.

On top of all that, he's got a reputation for being
quite a ladies' man. Since we spend a large part of our
time thinking about girls, we figure it can't hurt to have a
guy on our team who has pretty good access to them.

Once again, however, Deshutsis is firmly shaking his
head.

"Stoner," he says. "Thor Hupf is a partier and a pot-
head."

"He's not that bad," Beaterson says. "He maybe
hangs around with some shady characters, but—"

"Yeah, he hangs around with Savage, for one,"
Deshutsis says.

"So do we," Beaterson says.

"Besides," Deshutsis says, "he's a womanizer."

"We already agreed that's one of his best qualities,"
Beaterson says.

"No, he abuses women. He treats them shabbily."

Beaterson lets out a laugh. "Doobite, you're classic.
You are officially a card-carrying member of the pussy-
whipped male feminists."

"What do you mean by 'women'?" I ask Deshutsis. "You mean girls or old ladies at the bowling alley or what?"

"I mean our female classmates. He uses them and then discards them after he's gotten what he wants out of them."

"Dwight, you're scaring us," I say. "I think you need to go out and stand on the balcony."

"I do not need to stand on the balcony."

"Well, you sound like you're talking from personal experience or something," I say. "You sound like you're one of the women he's discarded."

"I just happen to know some women he's damaged."

"Damaged," Beaterson says. "I love it!"

"Like who?" I say.

"Like, oh . . . Dawn Cloos."

"Okay," I say, nodding. "Now this is starting to make sense. I thought you'd gotten over Dawn Cloos. You're jealous."

"I wouldn't say exactly . . ."

"Thor went out with Dawn Cloos a few times, long after she turned you down," I say.

"Thank you for reopening that wound. Thanks."

"All right, look," I say. "You don't want Summerfield. You don't want Thor. You definitely want to get rid of Savage. So, who do you want? Give us a name."

Deshutsis smiles.

"I've got the perfect solution. He's our age. He just moved into the apartments about three weeks ago. I've played pool with him a few times—I'm sure I've mentioned him to you. He's a heck of a nice guy. Tim Goon."

Beaterson and I look at each other, and immediately say no.

"We're not going to complicate things by bringing on somebody we've never even met," I say.

"I've met him," Deshutsis says.

"You don't count," Beaterson says. "You can't be trusted. You have zero credibility. How many times have you wanted us to meet some new dork you've dug up somewhere, and he's turned out to be a doofus?"

"I admit I've made a few mistakes in the past," Deshutsis says. "But Goon's not a doofus, I guarantee it. He's in good shape, drives a late-model Subaru wagon, and he loves football."

"We don't want to make new friends," I say.

"That's been our problem all along," Deshutsis says. "If we'd been more open to meeting new people and trying out new prospects after Glen died, we'd have been back to a five-man roster right away, with a couple of solid people on the waiting list. But no. Look at us. We have to scramble around at the last minute, and it's our fault, all three of us, because we're so damn picky about who we associate with. We have such a damn intolerance for anybody different from ourselves. We need diversity."

"I knew you'd say that word," Beaterson mutters.

"Look, all I'm saying is, let me pick up the phone, tell him to be at the cabana in three minutes. We walk over there, give him a mini-tryout. He's a quality guy. Trust me. How can it hurt?"

"It can hurt big," Beaterson says. "I still have nightmares about some of the losers you've introduced us to."

"I have to agree with Beaterson," I say. "We can't trust you. You mean well, but you have a warped judgment when it comes to new people. You exaggerate about them, and you even flat-out lie, because you want us to like them. We're going to vote you down on this, Dwight. I'm going to give Thor a call and see if he's available."

I've got Thor's phone number in my address book, and when I call him, he sounds stoned. He says he just woke up from a nap. When I tell him we're thinking of maybe adding another man to our roster, he seems interested.

Unfortunately, he has plans tonight. He's going to meet up with some friends at the football game at Memorial Stadium. Tomorrow, he's booked solid; he's working a six-to-ten morning shift at the doughnut shop, then heading to the Seattle Center as a representative of our school's Science Delegation, to participate in the Junior Science Symposium. I've never heard of the Science Delegation or the Junior Science Symposium, and for a second I'm tempted to ask about them, until I realize I don't care.

I ask him if any of this science stuff or his job at the doughnut shop would conflict with flag football, and he says no. He says he's willing to make flag football his number-one priority. And I believe him. The guy knows how to turn on the charm. No wonder he's successful with women.

Any way he can squeeze us in for an hour, just a quick tryout?

Okay, he says. How about tonight after the football game. Nine-thirty, south parking lot of the office park at WatchMark Technologies.

This is a good choice. It's got a big, well-lit parking lot that will be deserted on a Friday night, and lots of nice grass between the buildings that will catch ample light from the parking lot. A perfect place for a tryout.

"I think he's our man," I say, hanging up. "That guy is sharp as a tack."

But even as I say that, my stomach starts to feel lousy.

What about Cade . . .

As flawed as he is, Cade's given us a lot over the years, and he's our friend—he's one of us. And here we are, ready to give him the ax before we've even talked to him. But where is he? Why would he not even bother to contact me? He's asking for it.

Still, it seems like maybe we owe him more than this. He's not just our Oyster. He's like a brother to us.

Beaterson and Deshutsis are staring at me.

"You thinking about Savage?" Beaterson says. When I nod, he says, "Yeah, me, too."

"Don't you two start getting weak," Deshutsis says. "Savage is a mess."

"Yeah, but he's a familiar mess," Beaterson says. "He's a mess we know and love. On the other hand, Thor's a good guy. He's three times as good as Savage. We could win more games with Thor."

"You sounded too eager when you talked to Thor," Deshutsis says to me. "You sounded desperate."

"Look," I say, "I thought this was facing-reality time. We are desperate, and there's no use pretending we're not. The reality is, if we're going to dump Savage, then Thor or Summerfield are our only choices."

"They are not," Deshutsis says. "I've already told you who our best choice is, but you two won't—"

"Forget it," Beaterson says.

"We've been over that," I say. "Don't mention that name."

"I'll mention it and you can't stop me. Goon! Goon! Tim Goon! The Tim Goon Solution! Why don't you ever listen to me? I'm not asking you to go steady with the guy. Just meet him. We have time before we go meet Thor.

Goon's a decent athlete. Even more important than that, we can get along with him. He'll take orders from us. Yeah, sure, it would be nice to replace Savage with an improvement, but we don't want some hotshot coming along who thinks he's great and wants to start taking over, right? We want somebody who'll be subservient."

Subservient. An impressive word.

I have to admit, Deshutsis's displays of logic can sometimes be dazzling.

Sensing weakness, Deshutsis leans forward and licks his lips. "And there's one more thing about Goon I have failed to mention."

"I knew it," Beaterson says. "Here it comes. Okay, what's his deformity?"

"He's got a ski cabin."

Beaterson and I look at Deshutsis.

"Where?" Beaterson says.

"Crystal Mountain."

"And you just now happened to remember that?"

Deshutsis shrugs.

"You think he'd invite us?" I ask.

Deshutsis shrugs again.

I hand him the phone. "All right. We'll give him a look."

7

Outside in the fine, thin mist, we cut through the courtyard. This is an apartment complex of well-off retirees and yuppies, and very few kids. So we have pretty much free run of the pool, cabana, and weight room. I guess the retirees are too busy being retired, and the yuppies, when they're not working, prefer their own health clubs.

You can smell the damp woods that surround the apartment complex. The air here always seems a touch fresher and cooler than anywhere else.

TVs are flickering from living rooms all over the complex.

The cabana, with its big, wide picture window, is built on an elevated slope. The lighted walkway leads through a wrought-iron security fence and up some steps to the front door of the cabana. But Beaterson and I don't go for the door. Instead, we veer off the walkway and motor up the landscaped slope, between shrubs and bushes.

"What are you doing?" Deshutsis rasps at us from the walkway.

Beaterson and I cup our eyes and peer through the picture window.

"There he is," Beaterson whispers, as if Goon can hear us through the thick glass.

Goon is by himself, shooting pool.

"You guys ever hear of a thing called a door?" Deshutsis says. He's still down on the walkway, and he keeps checking over his shoulder, paranoid that the manager might come along.

Tim Goon's got this weird roadkill hairdo. It looks like it wants to be frizzy but he's shellacked it to his head.

And . . . he's dancing.

He's got the cabana stereo cranked up; we can hear the drums thump-thumping. They sound like they're going *Kennebunkport Kennebunkport.*

As Goon boogies around the table selecting his shots, he pivots and spins, gyrates his butt, and humps the air with his pelvis. Nodding his head to the beat, he looks right at us and grins. Beaterson and I duck instinctively, even though we know that he can't see us through the window. We've been in that cabana enough times at night to know that when it's dark outside, all you see when you look at the window is your reflection.

Beaterson and I are doubled over, laughing.

"What? What is it?" Deshutsis says. "What's so funny?"

We signal for him to come up and see for himself. At first he refuses, then curiosity gets the better of him and he chugs up the slippery bank.

"All right, he's dancing, so what?"

"Take a good look at that creature in there," I say.

Beaterson's on his knees. He's lost it.

"What's wrong with him?" Deshutsis says. "He's a well-built guy. You can see he's got coordination."

"He's wearing a silk shirt," I say. "With puffy sleeves."

"So?"

"He's Wayne Newton," I say. "That's Wayne Newton in there. And he's got breasts."

"He doesn't have breasts!"

"Look at his chest, Dwight. Those are jigglers."

"They're not!"

Beaterson is weeping with laughter.

"You're sick, both of you," Deshutsis says in a harsh whisper. "You're both hopeless. You're pathetic. Look at us, standing out here. You're bigots."

"We're biased against boys with breasts," I say.

"He's a loser," Beaterson says, recovering himself and wiping his face. "Let's get out of here."

"Who are the losers?" Deshutsis says. "Who are the losers? Huh? Who are the pathetic ones?"

Beaterson and I slide and scramble our way down the slope, leaving skid tracks.

Deshutsis catches up with us on the walkway.

"He's a nice guy! So what if he's dancing? What's wrong with letting go of your inhibitions when nobody's around?"

"I like my inhibitions," I say over my shoulder. "I don't want to let go of them."

"Same here," Beaterson says.

"I'm going in," Deshutsis says. "I called him. He's expecting us. We can't just leave."

"I wouldn't meet that guy in there if you paid me," Beaterson says.

"We don't need another loser at this point in our lives," I say.

Deshutsis stops following us and stands with his hands on his hips. "You've come this far and you're not even going to meet him. I don't believe it."

Beaterson and I turn down the path to the parking lot.

"Chickens! Gutless wimps! I've had it with both of you. I wash my hands of you. You disgust me. Bigots!"

A few minutes later, Deshutsis shows up in the parking lot. Beaterson and I are leaning against Deshutsis's Daewoo, which is parked between Beaterson's car and my car.

The good thing about Deshutsis, the good thing about all of us, is that we know which battles to fight to the death and which ones not to. It's one reason why we make such a good team and have managed to stay best friends since first grade.

"Did you go in?" I ask Deshutsis.

"No. What am I supposed to say to him?"

"Your turn to drive," Beaterson says.

Shaking his head, Deshutsis unlocks his door.

I take the front seat. Deshutsis tells us to wipe our muddy shoes with the towel he keeps for that purpose, which we never do and don't do now. He is so obsessive about keeping his car spotless, it's like he's got some kind of Daewoo cleanliness anxiety disorder. It always smells like aftershave—he keeps a bottle in the glove compartment and pats it on whenever he feels the need.

His driving style is nervous with frequent mirror adjustments. He keeps his sun visor down day and night, and there's a little mirror on it that he uses to check his zits when he thinks no one is looking.

"The problem with you two is that you fear and hate mankind," he says.

"We don't fear and hate mankind," I say. "We just don't want to meet a boy with breasts."

"I've spent time with him," Deshutsis says. "His body's as normal as yours and mine."

"You cop a feel every now and then?" Beaterson says

from the backseat. "When he's leaning over the table to take a shot?"

"You're trying to rattle me," Deshutsis says. "Go ahead, try all you want. You can't rattle me. Nope. No way."

He turns off the main highway and takes the long route up a side street, past the cemetery where Glen is buried. By force of habit we often drive by the cemetery, and observe silence, although it's okay to leave the radio or stereo on if there's a good song playing.

Leaving the cemetery behind, Deshutsis drives through familiar Seattle neighborhoods, eventually hooking back up with the main arterial, which takes us through a series of busy intersections, any one of which might bring us alongside somebody we know from our high school, going to or from somewhere on this Friday night.

Maybe a carload of cute girls.

You see cute girls just about anywhere you look, if you make it a priority and have eagle eyes, which we do.

We each have our own way of acknowledging the sight of cute girls.

Deshutsis whinnies like a horse and then makes a clicking noise in his throat, which he says he inherited from his grandfather, who, according to Deshutsis, claimed that when he used it on dogs he could literally drive them insane.

Beaterson sticks out his long tongue and makes a flicking, waggling motion with it, sometimes accompanied by a gurgling sound. It's pretty obscene.

Savage makes a short, high-pitched barking noise: "*Aow.*"

My trademark is a deep inhalation through clenched teeth, which I stole from John Lennon in the song "Girl." If you listen to the song, you'll hear it.

A common fantasy of ours is that someday a carload of cute girls will beckon us to follow them to their cabin on a remote country lake, and we'll all go skinny-dipping. And there will be no mosquitoes or adult supervision.

Cade Savage claims this happened to him last Fourth of July. He swears it's true. He's even driven us to the lake and shown us the house, which he says belongs to one of the girls' grandparents. But there's just no way it could be true. I mean, what are the odds of something like that actually happening to any of us? It's like winning the lottery. I wish I could believe whatever he says, but it won't be the first whopper he's told about himself.

If it were Beaterson or Deshutsis who said it, I would believe them. Lying is something Beaterson is just not capable of, period. And Deshutsis, even though he's a storyteller and a fabricator, doesn't tell lies to make himself look good or put himself in the starring role; he just twists the truth. He's always got some new urban legend.

Like the one about the well-known Seattle news anchor-woman who's a compulsive shoplifter. Or the one about the gang members who drive around at night with their headlights turned off, and the first car that flashes them, they hang a U-turn, drive up alongside the car, and start shooting. Everybody knows that's an urban legend, yet Deshutsis swears that it's true—he says it's a gang initiation rite. So whenever Beaterson or Savage or I see a car at night coming toward us without its headlights on, we say, "Oh, no! Gang initiation!" and flash our headlights at it. And so far, nobody's hung a U-turn and chased us down. But Deshutsis says one of these days our luck is going to run out.

I guess Cade Savage has always been the odd man out. With Beaterson, Deshutsis, and me, there's always been a cohesiveness. As for Glen Como, he was just plain different, an outsider by choice. Glen's fading more and more in my memory, and I suppose in a few more years I'll hardly think about him. But Glen was great, because he was so darn sure of himself and he made all the decisions.

It seems like Cade can't have fun anymore unless he's high or drunk. Beaterson, Deshutsis, and I have fun no matter what we do. We have this game we play sometimes, when we see a pretty girl. It's called Suicide. First we do a quick paper-rock-scissors competition, and the loser has to go up to the girl and ask her for her phone number—a suicide mission for sure. The beauty of the game is that you know you'll get shot down, so there's no pressure. Actually, the funnest part of the game is not in committing suicide—it's in the paper-rock-scissors contest to see who loses.

It's always nice to have an excuse to do something crazy like that, something we normally wouldn't do. I suppose that's the main purpose of getting drunk. Beaterson, Deshutsis, and I must be developmentally arrested, because for some strange reason, we just don't go near booze, and we hate going to parties where there's drinking. This avoidance of alcohol no doubt gets in the way of our growing up and becoming men. Maybe one of these days, with a little more maturing, we'll actually start acting our age and getting drunk and going to keggers. Then we'll really start having fun! We'll lose our inhibitions and not fear mankind. We'll yell and whoop and stagger around. We'll interact with girls. The ultimate will be that we'll wake up one morning in bed next to a girl we don't know, not remembering how we got there, realizing we've had sex with a total stranger. Then we will have arrived! We'll finally be men.

"It gave me the shivers," Beaterson says.

"Drop it," Deshutsis says, still driving.

"What a sight," Beaterson says. "Mincing around the

pool table like that. What a weird person. You're weird for suggesting him."

"You're not rattling me," Deshutsis says.

"I think you should have taken a left back there," I say.

"He was too busy not being rattled," Beaterson says.

"Just shut up, Beaterwipe, would you?" Deshutsis says.

"Boy," Beaterson says, "you can dish it out, but you sure can't take it."

We pull into the deserted campus of WatchMark Technologies and drive to the south parking lot. The streetlights cast an orange glow, and there's mist falling on the wet, glistening cement.

Thor's black van sits by itself in a corner of the parking lot. There's a pink-tinted dome light glowing from the inside, shining through the round porthole on the van's side panel. The superwide tires and chrome mags on the van probably cost more than my entire Ford Escort.

I get out and approach the van. I smell cigarette smoke.

For some reason, I'm leery about looking in the porthole of any van, let alone a van belonging to a known ladies' man. Instead, I clear my throat loudly, knock, and announce my name.

"Come in, come in," says a girl's voice.

Not exactly sure I want to, I open the rear door.

Inside, three girls are sitting cross-legged in a triangle on the shag rug that's on the floor of Thor's van, in a cloud of pink-lit cigarette smoke. They're wearing tank tops that show off skinny bare arms and smooth shoulders and throats.

We all say hello.

Their faces look familiar. They must be freshmen in my school. School's been in session only a couple of weeks, so I don't know their names, but I think I've noticed them.

Especially the dark-haired one with the bangs cut straight across her forehead, Cleopatra-style. Her eyebrows are dark. She's looking at me with a straightforward, intelligent smile. Her two friends have fairer, longer hair and their smiles are more self-conscious.

All three girls are cute in a ninth-grade sort of way, which is as cute as you can get. I never used the word *cute* until I started eleventh grade and started noticing these incoming freshmen from middle school who are two years younger than I am. *Cute* is the only word for them.

But it's that dark-haired Cleopatra one, the least cute of the trio, whose face has the most character, and I can't look away from her.

But I do. I take in this van with its customized interior. Not only has Thor laid nice shag carpeting on the floor, he's lined the walls and ceiling with . . . fur?

"Where's Thor?" I ask.

They don't say anything. They give each other side-glances, as if they've hacked up Thor's body and hidden it with the spare tire, and gotten a kick out of it.

"He's gone," the dark-haired one finally says. Her posture and hair are straight, and she's wearing dangly Indian-type earrings that I associate with Arizona or New Mexico.

"Where'd he go?"

"He took off." She's evidently the spokesperson.

"Without his van?"

"Brilliant deduction."

Her friends laugh. So do I. It was a good delivery.

"So he just went running off into the night?" I say.

"No, some guys in two cars followed us from the game and he went with them."

"Is he coming back?"

"Oh, yes."

Beaterson and Deshutsis have gotten out and are peering in. Deshutsis is looking over my left shoulder, but Beaterson isn't quite tall enough to look over my other shoulder, so he stands next to me, bouncing the football against his forehead.

"What have we here?" he says. "A love nest?"

"No love nest in here," the spokesperson says.

"No Thor in here, either," I say. "You guys sure you didn't murder him and dump his body in the woods?"

"We would have kept his keys," the dark-haired one

says. "Thor said if we waited here, you might give us a lift."

"Yeah?"

"He said to tell you he had to go do a couple of things but he'd be back pretty soon. Probably by the time you give us a lift."

"Where're you going?" Deshutsis asks.

"Robin Hood Lanes."

"Bad choice," Deshutsis says.

"Why?"

"It's gone down the tubes. It's not a place for serious bowlers."

"Like we're serious bowlers."

"Who were the guys Thor went with?" I ask.

All three of the girls start talking now, taking turns supplying information, finishing each others' sentences. Their timing is impeccable, like a three-headed anchorperson delivering the news.

They ran into Thor at the football game. They know him well enough to ask him if they could catch a ride to Robin Hood Lanes. He said sure, but first he had to stop off and meet some guys at nine-thirty about being on a flag-football team. So he drives them to this deserted parking lot. They're like, uh-oh, what have we gotten into here?

Next thing they know, Bao Alatina drives up in his new black sports car with another guy, followed by Cade

Savage in that muscle-car of his. They're all drinking beer. They talk to the girls for a while, and try to get the girls to go with them, but the girls say forget it, they're not that stupid.

So Thor says okay, you girls stay here in my van, catch a ride with the football guys, and tell them I'll be back around ten.

The girls pile into the backseat.

"Cute car."

Deshutsis gets in behind the wheel, and Beaterson sits up front in the passenger seat. Leaving me to squeeze into the backseat with the three girls. I'm smushed next to the dark-haired one. I'll take it.

The car smells like rain and outdoors and cigarette smoke and aftershave, and there's the foreign, damp-hair smell of these three girls. They've put on their jackets.

"Please extinguish all smoking materials," Deshutsis says.

"How do you roll this window down?" the girl on the far end says.

"It's a power window, dipwad," says the one next to her. "What kind of car is this, anyway?"

"A Ferrari," Deshutsis says.

"Nice try."

Beaterson turns around. "You girls happy back there?"

"Happiness is a relative concept," says the one who didn't know how to roll the window down.

"Somebody hasn't extinguished their smoking material back there," Deshutsis says.

The girl in the middle takes a final drag and tosses her cigarette out the window.

"I don't approve of littering," Deshutsis says, "but I'll let it go this time."

The cutest of the three, the one who said happiness is a relative concept, is named Danette. The one next to her is Chalise, which I believe means suitcase in French (French being the only elective I'm taking this semester).

The dark-haired one next to me is Malibu. I've heard that name around school from time to time as far back as fifth grade, but I've never crossed paths with the person connected to it, and now here I am, not only crossing paths with her but scrunched beside her in the backseat of a Daewoo.

Our egos have been gratified: the girls know who we are without our having to introduce ourselves.

"Dwight, you're famous, did you know that?" Malibu says to Deshutsis, patting his shoulder with her hand, which has painted nails and at least one ring on every finger, including the thumb. "You're practically a household name."

"Why's that?" he says.

"Last year you baked cookies for Dawn Cloos."

"Oh," Deshutsis says. "That."

"Our whole middle school knew about it. Plus, Danette is Dawn's little sister."

"Hi," Danette says, leaning forward.

Deshutsis almost swerves off the road. "You're Dawn Cloos's little sister?"

"Yes, and I thought it was a really sweet thing to do."

"Thank you," Deshutsis says.

"A lot of people thought it was pretty bizarre," Chalise says. "But not us."

"And you," Malibu says, patting Beaterson. "You're Rick."

"The *P* is silent," Beaterson says.

The girls laugh. Needless to say, he has used that line before and will use it again.

"Rick Beaterson, also known as the Tom Cruise look-alike," Chalise says.

"A young Tom Cruise," Danette says.

"Yes," Chalise says, "there's definitely a resemblance."

Even in the dark interior, I can see that Beaterson is blushing.

"And you," Malibu says, turning to me. I can feel her cigarette breath on my face. "Flint McCallister. Your friend Cade Savage told me some very interesting things about you tonight."

"I wouldn't believe much of what he says," I say.

"He told me to give you a message. He said he knows you're mad at him but he's not mad at you for calling Thor. He said he knows you'll keep your word, so you won't go telling other people certain things about him. He said you're loyal to your old friends and you wouldn't go dumping somebody without hearing their side of it first. He said you're a great quarterback. And he said you're invited to the big party he's having tomorrow night, but he doubts any of you guys will come. And he feels bad about all this, but it's something he has to do."

Something inside me is sinking. "That's enough about Cade Savage," I say.

"That's quite a message," Beaterson says over his shoulder. "Lo and behold, we spend half the night wondering where the hell he is, and along comes a messenger, delivering the word of Cade Savage. My, my, how do you like that?"

Deshutsis says, "How *is* Dawn these days?"

The parking lot of Robin Hood Lanes is packed with people loitering and having tailgate parties. Music blares from car stereos. This used to be an okay place to bowl, but it's become a glitzy hangout for middle-schoolers and high-schoolers. For purists, serious bowlers like ourselves, the preferred place to go is the more blue-collar Sundowner Bowl.

We pull up to the curb and drop the girls off. They light up as soon as they get out, as if it's been killing them to be denied a smoke for the ten minutes it took to drive here.

"Good luck," Malibu says to me through my open window.

"Thanks," I say, not sure why she thinks I need luck.

"Um . . ." Malibu glances at her friends and then looks back at me. "You guys want to come and bowl a game with us?"

There is a gaping silence in the car. It seems to last for minutes.

Finally, Deshutsis mumbles something about it being pretty hard to find a parking place.

I add something about meeting Thor.

"Oh, well," Malibu says. "I just thought I'd ask. How about Cade's party? You going?"

"We're not sure," I say.

"We can think of better ways to spend our free time," Deshutsis says.

"You might meet some people there," Malibu says.

We nod our heads.

Malibu smiles and shrugs her shoulders and turns to join her friends.

We drive away, leaving the girls standing on the curb.

9

We're driving in silence. I don't know whether to call it thoughtful silence or stunned silence.

"Well, that was different," Beaterson says.

"Were they coming on to us or what?" Deshutsis says.

"Tom Cruise," Beaterson mutters. He reaches up and twists the rearview mirror around to look at himself.

"Unbelievable," Deshutsis says, shaking his head. "Dawn Cloos has a little sister. I didn't know that. Did I know that? She's a vixen. 'Little sister, don't you do what your big sister done.' "

I lean back and stretch my legs.

"Actually, that might have been interesting," Beaterson says.

"What might have been?" Deshutsis says.

"If we'd gone in there with them and bowled."

"Six people on one lane is too many," Deshutsis says.

"Yeah, and it would have been hard to find a parking place," Beaterson says.

"Somebody had to say something. Nobody answered her."

Beaterson turns around and looks at me. "How about it, Captain? Should we have gone bowling with them? Or should we go and give Thor his tryout?"

"I told you Thor was a flake," Deshutsis says. "You guys never listen to me. You should have listened to me about Goon. Admit it, you should have gone in the cabana and met him. I was right about the storm last night, too. I wasn't going to mention that."

"Funny how you're mentioning it, though," Beaterson says.

"We'd better give Thor his tryout," I say.

"You can't mean that," Deshutsis says.

"We're not the moral police," I say. "What Thor does on his own time is his business. We've come this far. We might as well go and see if he shows up."

"We should at least take our time getting back there," Deshutsis says. "Let Thor cool his heels and wait for *us* for a while."

"Maybe we should have gone bowling with those girls," Beaterson says. "Maybe it would have changed our lives."

Deshutsis pulls into the parking lot of a minimart.

"I'm going to call Tim Goon," he says. "I'm going to

apologize for not showing up, and I'm going to ask him if he'll still meet us for a tryout. What do you say to that?"

"Go ahead, we can always stand him up again," I say.

Deshutsis gets out and heads for the pay phone outside the minimart. He takes his car keys with him. Things like that drive me crazy about Deshutsis. It's a wonder he didn't roll up his window and lock his door.

Beaterson in the front seat lets out a long, thoughtful sigh.

My thoughts are muddled. Are we the moral police? Should we have gone bowling with those girls? Should we sign Thor? What kind of game is Cade playing with us? Maybe I should have called Rachel Summerfield. What if we changed our minds and went back and bowled a game with those girls? Is Cade daring us to dump him? What's this about his having a party? What if I were to go to his party and run into Malibu there?

Beaterson cocks his head; I can tell he's about to say something.

"You ever wonder if there's such a thing as angels?" he says.

"No."

Outside the minimart, Deshutsis is talking on the phone. His lips are moving very fast and he's nodding his head. He hangs up and starts walking back to the car, twirling his car keys on his finger.

"I'm going to get some caffeine," he says, sticking his

head in through the window. "Anybody want some caffeine?"

"Not me," I say.

"Not me," Beaterson says.

Deshutsis turns and goes into the minimart.

"He didn't say whether or not he got hold of Goon-Goon," Beaterson says.

"He was talking to somebody," I say. "It could have been Goon. Or it might have been Goon's mom. Mrs. Goon-Goon."

For some reason, this sets us both off laughing. I'm remembering the sight of Goon leering at his reflection in the window and bobbing his head to the music.

I stick my hand out the window. It's starting to rain.

"Why, do you think there are angels?" I say.

"I don't know, that business with Malibu about the messenger, that reminded me of something. You remember a week or so ago, we had a couple nice days? I drove out to the boonies and went for a hike, just me. I found this little grove, I guess you'd call it, or a meadow or whatever. Not a soul around. Birds chirping, squirrels, chipmunks . . . I was stretched out on the grass with my shoes and socks and shirt off, soaking up the sun. And I thought, man, this is heaven. I was really at peace."

He pauses and glances back at me, as if checking to see if I'm laughing at him.

"Yeah?" I say.

"So I'm lying there on the grass, and I see this angel. She comes walking out of the bushes. Don't laugh."

"I'm not. Go ahead."

"She comes out of the bushes, and she's got something for me. It's a piece of paper. She shows it to me but she doesn't let me have it. You know what it is?"

"What?"

"A football scholarship. A full ride. To a small college. Somewhere like Eastern Montana or Wyoming."

"A full ride, huh?"

"Yeah. Well, I thought, how could it be a football scholarship, considering the fact that I don't even play real football, only flag football."

"Did you ask her?"

"No. She went back in the bushes."

"Did you follow her?"

"No."

"So, then you woke up."

"No, it wasn't a dream. It was . . . I don't know what it was. Maybe a hallucination."

I can see Deshutsis inside the minimart, pumping coffee from a large thermos into his Styrofoam cup. It takes Deshutsis such a long time to do something like get himself coffee and cream. A long, involved process. Everything takes Deshutsis a long time. And you can never really see why. Watching Deshutsis is like watching the hands of a clock. If you stare at him, nothing changes; it's only when you look away from him for a while and then look back that you see any progress that has been made.

"Do you think there's any real point to our existence?" Beaterson says, facing forward.

"I go back and forth on that," I say.

"I think there's got to be a point," he says. "To us. To this. To everything. If there isn't . . ."

"Then it's a big crock," I say.

"Yeah, like a hallucination. That scares the hell out of me. It scares the hell out of me so much that I've been thinking . . . I don't know, maybe I'll start going to church or something. My sister's been going. I don't know."

"I suppose it wouldn't kill you," I say.

"You don't think it would be weird?"

"No."

"Do you think it would give me a little more certainty about there being a point to our existence?"

"No."

"I think it all has to add up somehow. Past, present, future. None of this 'just live for the here and now' crap. All the people who have ever lived and died and who haven't even been born yet, they all count. All the things you ever did in your life, all the things you didn't do, all the things you will do. It's all cumulus."

Cumulus. A Deshutsis word. I've noticed lately that when Deshutsis uses a new word, Beaterson will sometimes use it (often incorrectly) a day or two later.

74

"When you put it that way," I say, "it sounds kind of scary."

"I know. That's why I think it would help me to go to church."

Deshutsis finally returns with a gigantic coffee. He has carved a hole in the plastic lid that he can sip through.

"What are you guys talking about?"

"Whether there's any meaning to our existence," I say.

"There is," Deshutsis says.

"I'm glad we settled that," I say.

"I got ahold of Tim Goon. He's waiting for his dad to come pick him up. He's spending the weekend at his dad's. His parents just split up a month ago and sold their house, which is why his mom moved to the apartments. His dad moved to a new place on a private lake. Tim's going through a rough time. His life—all their lives—they've just been wrenched and turned upside down. Trashed. Anyway, he forgives us for standing him up. He wants us to come to his dad's tomorrow anytime after two o'clock. He's going to let us take turns riding his jet ski."

"He has a jet ski?" Beaterson says. "A cabin at Crystal and a jet ski?"

"Yeah. I told him we'd come on over and give it—give him—a tryout. He gave me directions to the lake. You ever heard of a Lake Actumber?"

"Actumber," Beaterson says, shaking his head. "What's an actumber?"

"Sounds like a cross between October and November," I say.

"Anyway," Deshutsis says, starting up his car, "he's definitely psyched about being on our team. He is ready, willing, and able."

10

Back in the rain-glazed parking lot of WatchMark Technologies, we sit in Deshutsis's Daewoo, a few spaces from Thor's van, waiting for Thor. I can't tell whether Deshutsis is deep in thought or just thoroughly savoring each tiny sip of his coffee, or both. It kind of makes me wish I'd gotten a cup after all.

"How long should we give him?" Beaterson asks.

"We've given him too long already," Deshutsis says. "This is beneath our dignity, waiting for him like this."

"We'll give him till eleven," I say.

There's a light, steady patter of rain falling.

"Those girls," Beaterson says. "They were cuties. I kind of got a kick out of them."

"Dawn isn't a smoker," Deshutsis says. "Her little sister must be the rebellious type. I don't see why everybody thinks it's so weird that I happened to bake cookies for a girl."

"I don't either," says Beaterson. "Except that it was

only one of the all-time weirdest things you've ever done in your entire weird life. It gives me the creeps just thinking about it."

"Everything gives you the creeps," Deshutsis says. "Everything outside your narrow experience."

"I didn't mean it as a cut or anything," Beaterson says.

"Oh, well, then, thanks for the warm fuzzy."

"It's just a fact that you have womanly tendencies. That's not a cut."

"Don't start with the womanly tendencies," Deshutsis says.

"Honest, I'm not trying to put you down. I'm just stating a fact. You have major womanly tendencies."

"Just because I baked cookies for a girl."

"That's a womanly tendency. So is wanting to make new friends."

"What about you? You like to barbecue. That's *cooking*, isn't it? Huh?"

"Barbecuing is manly. It involves big slabs of meat, preferably ones you killed yourself. Baking involves mincing about the kitchen in a frilly apron, taking prissy little peeks into the oven."

"Some of the world's greatest chefs and bakers are men," Deshutsis says.

"Men with womanly tendencies."

I close my eyes and try to tune this out, I've heard it

before. Actually, I kind of admire Deshutsis for what he did.

Dawn Cloos, captain of the volleyball team, is six feet tall, the same height as Deshutsis. Shy and soft-spoken, braces, kinky hair that looks like long strands of Top Ramen. Not much personality, she's like a plastic doll, which for some reason is the kind of girl Deshutsis is always attracted to.

Last fall, about ten months ago, he had quite a crush on her, and, in a fit of insanity, he baked her cookies on the eve of her big volleyball tournament and left them on her doorstep with a handmade card wishing her luck. The next day, there was a pep assembly at our school. Dawn, being captain, was asked to step up to the microphone and say a few words to the fans on behalf of her team. She thanked everyone for their support, promised they'd do their best and so on, and said she especially wanted to thank Dwight Deshutsis for the delicious cookies that he had personally baked. The student body erupted into cheers, hoots, and guffaws. Beaterson and I were sitting next to Deshutsis, who of course turned bright red and looked like he wanted to dive under the bleachers. But we, his teammates and loyal friends, instinctively knew that the best thing to do was pretend as though we were anything but embarrassed for him, so we cheered and slapped him on the back.

For the next few days, it became a cause célèbre at

school, with people offering their opinions, and then it was quickly forgotten. As with many things that originate in the high school, it must have filtered down to the middle school and caused a stir down there for a while.

Deshutsis eventually mustered up the nerve to call Dawn and ask her out. She turned him down flat. Either she was spooked by the whole thing, or he just wasn't her type.

"She sure fooled me," Deshutsis says, taking a sip of his coffee. "It's one thing for her to not respect a guy who bakes cookies for her. It's another thing to turn around and go out with Thor Hupf, a guy who'd have no appreciation for her best qualities. But, I'm not jealous. It was her loss. I just never had her pegged for being the kind who'd prefer Thor over me. I just don't know why I seem destined to be attracted to the kind of girls who like cavemen."

"Ug," says Beaterson.

We decide to get out and toss the football around for a while. We make trick catches: one-handers, sideline, over-the-shoulder, coffin-corner. Deshutsis licks his palms and rubs them together, and we tell him to knock it off.

"What time is it?"

"Eleven-fourteen."

"The hell with him," I say.

As we're walking to Deshutsis's car, we hear a high-powered engine and see headlights. A black Porsche Carrera GT drives into the parking lot, music blaring. Its convertible top is down. Alatina's behind the wheel, Jedi Swing is in the passenger seat, and, sitting in the small backseat, holding a beer bottle, is Thor Hupf.

"Oowwwwwwww!" Thor howls.

I look for Cade but he's not with them.

Alatina kills the music. "Hombres."

"Bao. How's it going?"

I'm not sure what nationality Bao Alatina is, something South American. He slicks his hair straight back and ties it in a ponytail that fluffs out. Jedi Swing gets out and claps his hands at Beaterson, wanting him to throw a pass. Beaterson heaves one. Jedi leaps and catches it, but makes it look more difficult than it is, the sign of an inferior athlete. Thor scrambles out of the car, flings his beer bottle onto the grass, and says, "I'm open! Hit me! Hit me!" Jedi chucks it, and Thor says, "If I catch this, it means I can drive my own—" The ball careens off his chest.

"Okay, Thor," Alatina says. "Give your keys to Jedi."

"One more chance," Thor says. "I am not drunk."

Still sitting behind the wheel of his Porsche, Alatina turns to me and smiles. "Been waiting long for Thor?"

"Too long."

"He's in no shape to drive. And it's not good to leave the van here overnight. Somebody come along, strip those mags."

"Where's Cade?" I ask Alatina.

"Oh, he's tied up. I don't suppose you'd be interested in sampling some exceptional homegrown weed with the option to purchase? No, I didn't think so."

"What do you mean, tied up?" I ask.

"We are having a party tomorrow night at Cade's house. It is going to be the biggest party. We are going to invite everybody, citywide, and have many kegs. We are going to charge six dollars for the guys—all they can drink. And for the ladies, only a dollar. Lots of boys, lots of girls. Everybody will be happy. You coming? Six dollars, all the beer and women you can handle."

"I'll give it some thought."

"Okay, but don't say no to everything, Flint. That's what Cade says you do, say no to everything."

"Baby!" Thor is shouting. "Oh, baby, I love this game!" He still hasn't managed to catch a pass. "Let's play some tackle," he says. "Tackle football is the only way to go! None of this pansy flag crap!"

"How about it?" Jedi says. "Wanna play some three-on-three?"

"Sure," Beaterson says. "But not tackle. We'll either play two-hand touch or flag. We've got some flags and belts in the equipment bag."

"Taggle!" Thor yells.

"Yeah, tackle," Jedi says. "Touch is for wimps."

"We don't play tackle," Beaterson says. "We have too much respect for the game of football to play tackle. Three-on-three tackle football is pure slop. Nothing more than wrestling, trying to drag down the ball carrier, missed tackles, and long open-field runs. It's like playing three-on-three full-court basketball. All you get is fast breaks and breakaways. Just slop."

"Couldn't have said it better myself," Deshutsis says.

"Maybe you guys are just too wimpy to play tackle," Jedi says. He has taken the ball from Thor and is tossing it up and down, up and down, smirking. "Maybe you guys just don't like to get hit. Hmm?"

"No, it's not a question of wimpiness," Beaterson says. "It's a question of respect for the game. If you want to play tackle, we'll play tackle. Only don't call it football. Call it free-for-all, chase the guy with the ball around and knock the crap out of him. Now, you've got the ball, Jedi, so you're it. Start running."

Beaterson charges him.

Jedi's eyes go wide and his mouth drops open, just like a cartoon character. He runs a couple of steps before Beaterson slams full-force into his stomach and drives him backward five, ten, fifteen yards, off the parking lot and onto the grass, where Beaterson finally flattens him. The football squirts out of Jedi's hands and wobbles away.

Beaterson gets up. Jedi stays put.

Thor is staring with his mouth hanging open. "Two-hand touch," he says, nodding. "I'm willing to go two-hand touch. Or flag. Flag would be fine."

Alatina is laughing. "What do you say, Flint? Come to the party tomorrow night. Hey, how about those three freshmen you found in Thor's van, eh?"

"How about them," I say. "Where'd you say Cade is now?"

"I told you, he's planning his party. He doesn't want to think about football right now, Flint. He only wants to think about his party."

"Why doesn't he just tell me that himself?"

"Well, you know Cade better than I do. But you know what I think?"

"What?"

"I think he's one mixed-up midget."

Beaterson is helping Jedi up.

"Come on, Jedi, we got to go," Alatina calls. "Thor, hurry up and give him your keys. Rick, we needed you out there on the football field for our team tonight, man. We lost the game thirty-one to six. Or was it thirty-six to one?"

Taking the keys from Thor, Jedi limps over to Thor's van and gets in behind the wheel. Thor, before he climbs into the passenger side, mumbles some apologies to me. Alatina, alone now in his Porsche, guns it a few times before peeling out. It's the first time I've ever seen a Porsche go from zero to fifty out of a parking lot, and it's pretty impressive.

Thor's van follows at a leisurely speed.

Deshutsis and I walk over to Beaterson and take turns shaking his hand.

"Nice hit," I say.

"Helluva hit," Deshutsis says.

Beaterson tries not to look pleased.

11

We drive around for a while, not exactly sure what to do next. I'm in the front seat, and Beaterson's in the back. Deshutsis is still sipping his coffee, which must be ice-cold by now. We consider going back to Robin Hood Lanes and perhaps running into those girls. We can't think of a good reason *not* to go, except that we don't really want to go.

"Maybe we should force ourselves to do things we don't want to do," Beaterson says. "Maybe we need to force ourselves to do something new and unexpected. Diversity."

"What do you think I've been saying for so long?" Deshutsis says.

"Then, why don't you want to go back to the bowling alley?" Beaterson says.

"Because . . . ," Deshutsis says, but the word just hangs there.

"Flint, what do you think?" Beaterson says.

"I think we've got other things to worry about right now," I say. "I'm going to have to cancel two practice games tomorrow."

"What a waste," Beaterson says. "We should be spending this weekend fine-tuning our offense and defense."

Deshutsis is driving through some quiet streets. I'm not paying much attention to where he's going.

"There's something I've been meaning to bring up," Deshutsis says. "This might not be the best time for it. But I at least want to raise the issue for general discussion."

"Isn't he cute when he wants to raise an issue?" Beaterson says.

"What is it?" I say.

"Well, I don't want you to get offended," Deshutsis says to me. He takes a tiny sip of coffee.

"What is it?"

"You won't get offended?"

"Just tell me what it is."

"I think we should consider changing our team name. I mean, as long as Jeff is going to let us replace Savage with a new player, then let's change our name, too, and make a whole new start. Does that—do you take umbrage at that?"

He must think it will hurt my feelings because Glen Como came up with the name, and, of course, everything Glen Como did must be sacred, because he's dead.

"Change it to what?" I say.

"Well," Deshutsis says, clearing his throat, "we can toss some ideas around, of course. This might not be the best time, but I just wanted to see if you are—to see if you're amenable to a name change, that is, to the possibility of breaking tradition, so to speak."

Amenable. Umbrage. Jesus, where does he dig up these words? Does he collect them or what?

"I like tradition," I say. "It's bad luck to change our name."

"I know you respect tradition. So do I. But sometimes it's good luck to change. We ought to be more progressive. More proactive. Rather than not do something because we're afraid it'll be bad luck, we ought to do something new and different because we think it will be good luck. It's good luck to dump Savage. It's good luck to change our team name. If you get mired in tradition, that's bad."

"What's wrong with Three Clams and an Oyster?" I say.

"It's too long. It ought to be short and sweet. Just one word. It ought to be something sort of uplifting and positive, inspiring. It would gain us more recognition, more respect and attention. Something like, oh, I don't know, Glory. Or Spire. Or New Beginnings. Or Growth."

"Growth?" I say.

"Growth?" Beaterson says.

"I'm just brainstorming."

"Growth?" Beaterson says again.

"Just forget it," Deshutsis says.

"Consider it forgotten," I say.

"I mean, if you don't want to brainstorm . . . ," Deshutsis says.

"I think that's enough brainstorming for one night," I say.

Deshutsis drives along. I wish I were in the backseat so I could stretch my legs out sideways.

"Can I just make one more point?" Deshutsis says.

"I don't think we can stop you," I say.

"The real problem with our team name, you see, it's exclusionary It's like, the Oyster, the fourth man, he's not part of the unit. He's separate from the Three Clams. That was okay for Glen—he wanted it that way. But with Savage, I think it's always made him feel like the odd man out. Better to have a name that makes all four of us a single solid entity. A—a—"

"Don't say that word," Beaterson says.

"A fusion."

"Agh!" Beaterson says, rocking back. "I told you not to say it!"

"You really think that's true about Savage?" I say. "You think he feels excluded?"

"Of course. Nothing but a cheap substitute for Glen Como. The guy who he indirectly killed. No wonder it's taken its toll on Savage. You *know* he thinks that."

"Then maybe we ought to talk to him about that," I say. "Maybe we need to remind him he's one of us."

Deshutsis shakes his head. "It's too late for a heart-to-heart talk. You'd just sound desperate, like you're begging him to straighten up and behave himself. We can't really trust him. Besides, he's always been our weakest link. It's time to get somebody sane. Somebody respectable, who'd look good in the eyes of a sponsor. Somebody like Tim Goon. Let Savage go. Cut him loose. He's on the road to hell."

"It would be kind of nice to get somebody who'd make us more competitive," Beaterson says.

"Summerfield?" I say.

"Maybe we should give her a shot," Beaterson says, leaning forward.

"You know my doubts about Summerfield," Deshutsis says.

"You afraid you're going to bake cookies for her?" Beaterson says.

Deshutsis ignores this.

"What if she can make us win?" Beaterson says. "And just think how attractive she'd be to a sponsor. I've got an idea. Instead of Three Clams and an Oyster, we can call ourselves Six Testicles and a Vagina."

"That's not funny at all," Deshutsis says. "That's sick. And that's exactly the reason why we shouldn't have a female on our team. Because you can't handle it."

"Aw, come on, let's at least give her a tryout," Beaterson says. "We'll still take a look at this Goon idiot tomorrow. I say we do it."

"It won't hurt to give her a call and see if she's available," I say.

Deshutsis raises his hands from the steering wheel in surrender. "Okay. Okay. Probably a mistake, but call her."

We find a pay phone. Beaterson and Deshutsis get out and watch as I dial her number. Eleven-thirty on a Friday night, this might not be the best time to call.

Her mother answers and doesn't sound too pleased. A few seconds later, Rachel's on the line. I tell her who I am and start to explain the situation.

"Yes," she says, interrupting me somewhere during "we were wondering if you'd." "The answer is yes."

"It would just be a tryout," I say. "No guarantees. We've got some other—"

"All I want is a tryout," she says. She has kind of a hoarse, brusque voice. "I'd like a shot. I've been home all evening. I jump rope ten minutes every night."

"That's impressive."

"I've wanted to be on a four-man flag-football team for two years," she says. "But I never could find the right fit. I don't want to play on a girl's team—they have different rules for females."

I make eye contact with Beaterson and Deshutsis, who are staring at me quizzically, trying to figure out what on earth she's saying to me.

"I'd even do it tonight if it were a little earlier," she says. "But I have a rugby match in the morning. Oh, and don't worry about the rugby, I'm just filling in for a girl who's injured—it's just a one-time-only thing. I can meet you tomorrow either before or after the rugby match, but before would be better, because they'll want to go out for pizza after the game. How about nine? Would that be too early?"

"No, that'll work," I tell her.

She gives me directions to the rugby field. After I hang up, I look at Beaterson and Deshutsis.

"Man," I say. "She's focused."

12

We *rendezvous* the next morning at Deshutsis's apartment complex. Today we are taking Beaterson's car. A huge gas-guzzling, road-hogging 1970 Buick LeSabre. Bench seats, front and back, so big and roomy you can almost fit Deshutsis's Daewoo in it.

Beaterson's been trying to get us to call his car "the Beaterbuggy." "Call it the Beaterbuggy," he will say from time to time. "Say, 'Let's take the Beaterbuggy.'" But Deshutsis and I can't do it. If a nickname doesn't come naturally, there's no use trying to force it.

As we head south to the rugby field, Beaterson and Deshutsis want to know how I survived my first night on my own. They're disappointed when I tell them the only time I was frightened was when I first walked inside; it took me a couple of seconds to remember that I'd spent two and a half hours cleaning the house earlier that day.

First thing this morning I had to call the captains of the two teams we were scheduled to play practice games against today and cancel. They were not pleased. I can only hope we'll be able to salvage the two we've still got scheduled for tomorrow.

"I had a talk with my sister last night," Beaterson says.

Beaterson's sister Sari is one of the wisest people we know. Whenever he talks to her, he always comes away with some new insight.

"She thinks we should utilize tough love on Savage."

"She said *utilize*?" Deshutsis says. He's in the backseat this morning, rolling one of the two footballs over his thighs. "Anytime your sister uses the word *utilize*, she should be listened to. And anyway, she's saying exactly what I've been saying. Of course, you listen to her and not me. Isn't it interesting how I always make more sense after you talk to Sari."

"Is it just me, or is he more of a dick in the morning than at other times of the day?" Beaterson says to me.

"While we're on the subject of dicks," Deshutsis says, "I don't think anyone ever adequately acknowledged how right I was about Thor yesterday."

I ignore Deshutsis. "So your sister thinks we should dump Savage?"

Beaterson nods. "She says the worst thing we could do would be to give him another chance. You need to go talk to him."

"I do? Why me?"

"You're our captain, for one thing. But you're also closer to him than Dwight or I are. It'll be kind of a delicate operation. You have to throw his ass off the team, but at the same time, you have to tell him—you know, without being all sappy about it—that we still care about him, and that's exactly why we're throwing his ass off the team."

"I still don't see why we all can't go and tell him that," I say.

"We don't want it to turn into some kind of a love fest," Beaterson says. "Talking to somebody one-on-one is better than all of us ganging up on him. He's different around Dwight and me—he puts on more of a swagger. And anyway, Dwight and I can go and see him separately later on in the week. For now, though, you should be the one to dump him."

"Agreed," Deshutsis says.

"I don't know," I say. "He'll be all hungover Sunday morning. If I go and dump him, it'll be like kicking him when he's down."

"That's tough love," Beaterson says.

"That's right," Deshutsis says. "Sometimes you have to kick them when they're down, in order to enable them to pick themselves up by themselves. That just came to me. That sounded incredibly wise and poetic. Somebody should write that down."

We pass Husky Stadium and cross the Montlake

Bridge, then take a left and drive through the Arboretum, which is exploding with fall colors. We continue south, through the Central district, past Rachel Summerfield's big brick high school. We don't have far to go now.

"I'll give you another tip my sister gave me last night about girls," Beaterson says. "This is the big one, according to my sister. The number-one key to success. Now, let's say you're at a party, and you—"

"We don't go to parties," Deshutsis says.

"All right, say you're at some other function where there are girls."

"When was the last time that happened?"

"Don't heckle me," Beaterson says. "It seems like we had a chance last night."

"Let's hear what the key is," I say.

"Why should I bother? Dwight's right. Every time we get in a situation with some girls, we turn and run."

"Last night wasn't a good time," I say. "We're right in the middle of a crisis."

"True," Beaterson says. "All right. Let's say we're at a party. Say we're at Savage's party, for instance."

"A kegger?" Deshutsis says.

"Why not. Say you see some girl you'd like to get to know. You go over and you strike up a conversation with her. The key is—here's the key: eye contact. You have to maintain steady eye contact. My sister calls this 'the Hungarian Method.' Because Hungarians—like Dracula, for instance—are masters at utilizing this constant, hypnotic eye contact. You just keep your eyes glued on the girl's while you're having this conversation with her. You don't look around, you don't let your eyes shift, you keep your eyes *riveted* on hers."

"Both eyes?" Deshutsis says.

"What do you mean, both eyes?"

"Can you let one eye wander around while the other eye remains fixed on her?"

"Why don't you shove it."

"Dracula wasn't even Hungarian," Deshutsis says. "I don't even think there is a Hungary anymore. I believe it was absorbed into Greater Actumber."

"Why do I waste my time," Beaterson says.

Eventually we find a big parking lot that's adjacent to several fields. There aren't many cars here. We put on our cleats and jog out to the field and start tossing the football.

What a beautiful thing it is, grasping a football that's slightly wet with dew and throwing a high, arcing spiral through the air and watching somebody catch it, and then having them throw it to you, and you reaching up and catching it in your fingertips. With autumn bursting everywhere. Colors, smells. Way off in the distance, there's the echoing sound of hammering. Somebody doing it the old-fashioned way, one nail at a time.

Suddenly, I feel a wave of happiness. It's more than

the exhilaration of getting out on the field and throwing the football around. It's a kind of gratitude and contentment. Like when Beaterson found himself in that peaceful grove and thought he saw an angel. Maybe I'll see an angel. Maybe luck will come my way. I'd like a good dose of luck.

The distant hammering stops, leaving silence. I stand with my hands on my hips, feeling the cool, misty air on my face, watching the football soar against the sky.

13

A *beat-up,* boxy car enters the lot and parks. Rachel Summerfield gets out. I like the car. It looks like something she bought with her own money.

She jogs up to where we're standing. Her face is flushed. She's wearing a green and gold rugby uniform. Her hair is just above her shoulders, kind of deer-colored; some of it is pinned back from her face and forehead. She's not wearing any makeup, but her skin is so smooth and healthy-looking, it seems to glow.

When I ask her how she's doing, she smiles and says she's a little nervous. Her husky voice sounds the way most people's do when they have a cold, but hers is always that way.

"Nervous about the rugby or this tryout?" I ask.

"Nah, the rugby's just for fun. No—it's this. This morning I woke up, I swear I thought I'd dreamed that phone call from you. I had this dream that I got a job as a gift-wrapper in a store, and on my first day of work . . ." Her voice trails off.

"Your first day of work?" I say.

"Never mind. It's boring to hear about someone's dream."

"No, go ahead," I say.

Beaterson and Deshutsis are looking at her with a strange blankness. I know those expressions; there is horror below the surface. What have they seen, after only one minute, that has spooked them?

"Well," she says, smiling, "in the dream, I was supposed to work from two in the afternoon till six in the evening. My first day of work. And I didn't show up. I just forgot I was supposed to be there."

"Ha ha ha," I fake-laugh.

Beaterson and Deshutsis aren't even smiling, although they probably think they are.

There is an awkward silence. I want to say something to lighten things up and put Summerfield at ease. But forced small-talk is one of those weird rituals; it would probably only heighten the discomfort level.

Beaterson and Deshutsis aren't helping. Maybe they have the right attitude. They're not trying to be polite or friendly; they're not pretending to be anything. We'll either hit it off or we won't, and there's no point in—

Then I notice her legs.

They're not shaved.

My knees buckle. My crotch goes all tingly.

Obviously, this is what Beaterson and Deshutsis have already noticed.

I recover, scan the sky for airplanes and cloud formations. It doesn't bother me. Heck no. It just caught me a bit off guard. I look over at Beaterson and Deshutsis and notice they're searching the same sky. I must reestablish eye contact with Summerfield. The best I can do is look at her scalp for a few seconds, then up at the sky.

In all the times I've seen her, I've never noticed hairy legs. And these are not downy or nubbly, they are old growth. I've played basketball with her at the rec center many times. Did she always wear long sweats? Possibly, but I don't think so. If she had worn shorts even once, I'm sure we would have noticed her legs. Which means, for some reason, she has stopped shaving them. Did something happen? Is she making a statement, experimenting with an alternate hygiene style, or what?

Her face, with that glowing, ruddy complexion, is just naturally pretty; and her body is great. It's absurd to be grossed out by one little . . .

I clear my throat and clap my hands twice. "Okay, let's get started. Why don't we do some shaving."

They all look at me.

"Stretching," I say. "Let's do some stretching."

Beaterson coughs and looks off to the side. Deshutsis watches a bird.

Summerfield and I get down on the damp turf and start doing whatever stretching routines we've picked up over the years. Beaterson and Deshutsis stand off to the side, each holding a Wilson football.

"So, uh, do you guys use a no-huddle offense?" Summerfield asks.

"No," I say. "We huddle."

"Oh? Why's that? I would think you'd just run it like a two-minute drill, using audibles from the line of scrimmage. Do you really have that much of a need to huddle-up in flag football?"

"Yes," I say.

She has her legs stretched out in a V and is working her groin muscles. That is, if girls have groin muscles—or groins.

"Why is that?" she asks.

"Well," I say, "you have to do a lot of improvising during a flag-football game. You have to adjust to what the defense is doing at that moment. We do have a lot of set plays, of course. We have a whole playbook full of them. But often we have to invent a play right on the spot, custom-made for the defense we're facing. And even then, when we break out of the huddle and line up at the line of scrimmage, I might decide to change the play and call an audible instead."

"What sort of audible system do you use?"

"It's pretty basic. You should be able to learn it pretty fast. It's a combination of colors, numbers, and syllables."

"How about defense? Zone or man-to-man?"

"Zone, usually. Beaterson makes the calls on defense. He's our defensive coordinator."

Summerfield looks over at Beaterson and gives him an impressed, pleasant smile. Her eyebrows have a sort of high arc to them, and her features all blend together harmoniously, making for a nice face. I sneak another quick look at her legs.

How do you ask someone you don't know very well, "What's with the legs?"

It really shouldn't matter.

And yet, if Beaterson or Deshutsis or Savage were to start *shaving* their legs, I would have no problem saying, "What's with the legs?" So I guess the question is, at what point do you feel comfortable enough with someone to say, "What's with the legs?"

She wants to show me some special stretches that she likes, but I've had enough stretching. I get up. I look over at Beaterson and Deshutsis. Why don't they interview her? Ask her about her hobbies or favorite music or something.

My God, have they already made up their minds to reject her?

Are we really that bigoted?

"Do you mind if I say something?" Summerfield says.

"No, go ahead."

"Well, it's just that I care about winning. I care a lot. And that's one reason why I refused to join up with most of the other teams who recruited me. I would rather sit out and not play at all than play on a team with people who aren't serious. Does that make sense?"

"You bet," I say.

She seems encouraged. "Have any of you ever been on a team that won a championship? I don't just mean in flag football, I mean in anything."

We all shake our heads.

"Well, I was in a soccer club back in eighth grade, and we won State. I'm not saying that to brag. But I learned something that year that you can only learn by being on a championship team."

"And what was that?" I say.

"When you're on a team that wins a championship, there's this magic that happens maybe midway through the season, give or take. There's a click. You hit this groove, where you realize you can read each other's minds, and the breaks start going your way, and you start doing incredible stuff that doesn't seem so incredible. You become this *team*, no longer a bunch of individuals with individual talents. You're totally focused, and yet there's never a sense of awe or amazement at what is happening. And I'll tell you, there's nothing like that. I want that again. That's what I want."

Her eyes seem to have brightened a notch or two.

I find myself saying, "Do you . . . think we could reach that level?"

"I believe so," she says. "I think there are only two teams who might be better than us. Marty's Texaco and The Doctor Lauras. But I think they're both beatable. I think we can win this division. I think we can get a sponsor. And if we get a sponsor, we can go to tournaments all over, all the way through summer. We can compile points and get a national ranking. Next year, when we're all seniors, we can go all the way to Nationals."

I feel as though I'm falling under her spell.

"How come you're not playing soccer this season?" I ask.

"Oh, that's a long story. The bottom line is I've been skiing a lot the last couple of years and playing a lot of basketball. I just lost interest in soccer, especially after eighth grade when our club broke up and we all went to different high schools. I got this bee in my bonnet, I wanted to play flag football. I just think—I just have this feeling—that I'm a natural-born flag-football player, especially four-man. I've tried seven-man, and I don't like it as much."

I think I could listen to her talk for another hour. I like the sound of her voice.

I ask, "Do you think your being a girl, and us being guys, do you think there'd be any problem with that? I mean for road trips and that sort of thing?"

"I've thought about that," she says, nodding. "I think if we're honest and up-front with each other . . . Look, we just need to be ourselves, that's the main thing. It might take time, but it'll happen. We need absolute, total permission to be ourselves. I mean, I know I probably act differently around girls than I do around guys. I'm probably more myself around girls, although I have a couple of guy friends, and I have an older brother and a younger brother, and I get along with both of them very well. I think we'll all be mature enough to handle it."

"Handle what?" Beaterson says. As if he's just been woken up from a nap.

"The gender issue," Rachel says.

I am a believer. I am suddenly, wholly, and completely a believer in Rachel Summerfield. She is absolutely genuine, the real thing. I feel like she understands us and believes in us. I've never felt that understanding and respect from anyone, except the rare fellow flag-football player.

And she wants to be on our team. That's the incredible thing.

Beaterson has a strained, constipated look on his face—I can't tell what he's thinking. But Deshutsis, he looks interested.

He clears his throat.

"I've been wondering something lately," he says in his professorial voice. "The thought has crossed my mind that there might be a problem with our name, Three Clams and an Oyster. You spoke just now about that unifying principle, that bond. A fusion, if you will. Do you think—I'd be interested to hear your opinion vis-à-vis our team name—that the Oyster feels alienated or disenfranchised because he stands alone in our name, and this name maybe doesn't give us the adhesive quality that we need?" He clears his throat again. "This fusion, if you will."

Beaterson emits a low growling noise from somewhere in his throat.

Summerfield blinks rapidly and looks contemplative. I'm curious if she has even the slightest idea what Deshutsis has just said.

"Oh," she finally says. "I love the name. Don't change it. I think it's perfect. Three Clams and an Oyster. There's an air of mystery to it—who's the Oyster and all that. And it's very Northwest, of course. It doesn't take itself too seriously, and yet it's not just a cheap joke. No, really, I think the name is perfect."

She nods her head a few times, then stops, and finishes with such a relaxed and natural smile that I feel good from my heels all the way up.

My God, she's a winner. As in the opposite of a

loser. She's won before and she can win again, knows how to win, expects to win. Wants to win. With us. Why us? How does she see us? I mean *us* as people. I'd like to ask her that. I bet she'd tell me, which makes me a little afraid. And yet she wants us. She'll make us winners.

But hold on, let's not get too carried away. We haven't even given her a tryout yet.

"Okay, let's start by having you hike the ball a few times."

I toss her the football. She turns around and bends over with both hands extended forward on the ball. I stand behind her, about twelve feet back. She looks at me upside down from between her legs. My heart sprints, and I have to settle my breathing. I don't dare look at Beaterson or Deshutsis.

I'm wondering if there is any way I can get used to standing behind Summerfield when she bends over to hike the ball. I suppose it's like Mount Rainier; in time, you learn to take the view for granted.

"Hike."

She snaps the ball back to me in a bullet. It hits my fingers, and I drop the ball.

She straightens up and looks at me over her shoulder. "Sorry, was that too hard?"

"No, that was fine."

I glance at Beaterson and Deshutsis. They are both smirking at me.

Beaterson, who's holding the second football, tosses it to Summerfield, and I flip the football I just dropped to Deshutsis. Using the two footballs in this continuous relay system, Summerfield gets in a rapid twenty-five or thirty hikes. Each one is chest-high, and faster than Savage was ever able to shoot at me. Those extra tenths of a second make a difference when you've got a guy on defense rushing you.

"All right, enough hiking," I say. "Let's throw you some passes."

In the same two-ball rotation, I have her run a series of ten-yard down-and-outs. She catches each pass, tosses the ball to Beaterson, runs another pattern, and catches my next pass, while Deshutsis covers her loosely on defense. Her hands aren't big but they're sure; she forms a flexible web and snags the ball in sticky fingertips. I purposely try to move the ball around—low, high, left shoulder, right shoulder, behind, in front. She catches them all and makes it look easy.

"Let's run some patterns," I say. She trots over to me and we huddle, face-to-face. Her cheeks are red and she's breathing hard, and her hair has beads of mist on it. I tell her to go down five yards, fake left, and go right.

She hikes the ball and runs the pattern precisely, making a good, crisp fake. I have her run buttonhooks, fake buttonhooks, sideline turn-ins, posts, everything I can think of. She fakes, cuts, zigzags. She's not afraid to dive for the ball. She's fast, quick, agile, well coordinated. And always like she's only using three-quarters' effort; like there's another one-quarter waiting in there for when she needs it.

That effortlessness is so rare. She has it when she plays basketball, too; she just doesn't even look like she's trying that hard at all. She doesn't waste steps or movements, doesn't try to force anything, never looks awkward or out of sync. Her movements are graceful and languid. I like the way she can improvise on a pattern to get open. I like the way she can shift into high gear and accelerate after she catches the ball. She's going to score touchdowns. McCallister to Summerfield—six points.

I have her play some defense, and she alternates between covering Beaterson and Deshutsis as I throw passes to them. Her defense is solid, just like it is in basketball. She can zigzag backward very quickly, mirroring the receiver; she's got an instinct for when to try for the interception and when to concede the catch and make the quick flag-pull.

She's passed every test I can think of. Just like she said, she's a natural; the consummate flag-football player.

Okay, so the only thing I'm wondering now is, what's the catch?

14

"What?"

"I said, will I ever get to throw the ball?"

The four of us have walked over to the sideline of the rugby field and sat down on the empty bleacher.

"Sometimes," I say. "We have some great flea-flicker plays and that sort of thing."

"I mean, quarterback," she says.

"What about it?"

"Will I ever get to play it?"

"You want to play quarterback?"

"Yeah."

"I'm the quarterback."

"All the time?"

"Yeah."

"Hmm," she says. "Is that negotiable?"

"Everything is negotiable," I say. "We're a team, and we want to be flexible and give and take."

"So, if we negotiate, I might be able to play quarterback sometimes?"

"No."

"Why not?"

"Because I'm the quarterback."

"But you said everything's negotiable."

"Yes. But we also need some consistency in our positions, you know? We've got thirty seconds to run a huddle. We can't go negotiating who's going to play quarterback on which down. We can't do everything by democracy. We can't go into the huddle and say, 'Okay, who wants to be QB this play?' "

"But," she says, hesitating, "do I have to hike the ball on every down?"

"You're an excellent hiker."

"Thanks, but . . . every down?"

"Traditionally, our Oyster hikes the ball every down, yeah. That's how it was with Cade Savage, and same with Glen Como, our Founder." I look over at Beaterson and Deshutsis. They are not going to say a word.

"Yeah, but . . ." Rachel frowns.

"We want everybody to be happy," I say. "You want to try different positions, we can make some adjustments as we go along during the season. We're not inflexible. But. You've got to learn our playbook by next Saturday. We have to get used to working together as a team. I'd just as soon you concentrated on one single position for a while."

Again I glance at Beaterson and Deshutsis.

This is what I don't tell Rachel:

Beaterson and Deshutsis hate hiking the ball. Hate it. I can't blame them. Hiking the ball is a hassle. It's a headache, not to mention a buttache and a backache. It makes you take your thoughts off the pass pattern you're about to run. It's a chore. You have to bend over. You have to grip the ball properly. You have to look at the QB upside down between your legs, which makes the blood rush to your head. You have to be responsible for making a good hike.

"Well," she says. "Gosh, I don't know. Can I speak my mind?"

"Sure."

"Well, I don't want to make a big deal out of it," she says. "I mean, I realize I'd be the newcomer and all that. But . . . this is going to sound conceited."

"Go ahead," I say.

"The way I see it, having me is going to add another weapon to your offensive arsenal, a dimension to your offense that you didn't have with Cade Savage, no disrespect to Cade or anything. I can run fast and I can run patterns that will get me open, and I think you should utilize my speed. It just seems like it would be a waste of me to have me hike the ball every single play, don't you think?"

Deshutsis speaks up.

"Hiking the ball is not a waste of time," he says. "It's

of vital importance. Delivering the ball to the quarterback is one of the most imp—"

"It's the job nobody else wants, so it gets dumped on the new guy," Summerfield says. "Like cleaning the toilets. That's of vital importance, too."

Deshutsis opens his mouth, but no words come out.

"What percentage of plays would you feel comfortable hiking the ball?" I ask.

"Well, there are four of us. We're a team, right? A single unit. If you divide a hundred percent by four, you get twenty-five percent each."

I stare at her.

"Give or take," she adds tentatively.

Deshutsis, his voice going up a notch, says, "This is a football team, not a commune. We're not going to divvy everything up in equal parts."

"Rachel," I say. "I'm the quarterback. I'm not going to hike the ball twenty-five percent of the time. Everybody has a role to play."

"The age of specialization, is that it?" she says. "All I want is just to play quarterback sometimes—every once in a while. I have a cannon for an arm."

"There's more to being a quarterback than throwing the ball," I say.

"I can read defenses. I can call plays. Look, you guys," Summerfield says, "I know you're thinking I'm coming on too strong. I'm not like this all the time, believe me. But I also have to stand up for myself. I'm not a doormat. Now, you guys are all good players, but let's face it, you're not superstars. Do you want to win or not? If so, you've got to have a bit more variety. Flint, you sit back there at quarterback every down, same guy hiking the ball every play, the defense likes that, it's predictable, one more thing they can take for granted. You shake them up, though, when you start shifting around and mixing up positions. I mean, I realize you guys are going to need some time to adjust to a new guy and all. I don't want to totally blow you out of your comfort zone on day one. But I don't know if I'd be all that contented being on a team that's predictable and set in its ways. I don't know if I'd be contented being on a team where I wasn't given an equal piece of the pie, especially since I'm at least equal or better in all the skill matchups."

"We're happy in our comfort zone," Deshutsis says.

"You think you are," she says pleasantly. "That's the tricky thing about comfort zones."

"I can't hike the ball," Deshutsis says, shaking his head. "It gives me a tension headache. I start to see stars, a whole spectrum of streaks and lights. It makes me dizzy."

"You'll adapt," Summerfield says.

"You're the newcomer," Deshutsis says. "Haven't you ever heard of paying your dues?"

Summerfield smiles. "The seniority system? What is this, the Teamsters Union?" She looks over at me, chuckling, wanting to share the laugh, but I'm studying grass blades. She says, "Seniority is a loser attitude, for dinosaurs, guys. Imagine somebody in professional sports trying to use that argument."

For the second time, Deshutsis opens his mouth and nothing comes out.

Beaterson squints off at the distant trees.

For the past few minutes, cars have been driving into the parking lot, and members of the the two rugby teams have been slamming doors and walking up to the sidelines of the rugby field.

"Well," Summerfield says, "I suppose I've torpedoed any hope I had. You guys probably think I'm too bossy and pushy. But if being the Oyster means being the doormat, I'd rather sit out the season and wait for skiing and rec basketball."

"We've got a couple of other people we need to look at today," I say. "I'll get back to you later."

She nods. "You can always reach me on my cell phone. Can I ask you a big favor?"

"Sure."

"Let me know as soon as possible? Waiting just drives me crazy. That helpless feeling of expecting the phone to ring, only it doesn't ring. I mean, it just drives me crazy when something isn't in my own power, you know what I mean? I'd rather you just told me no right now than drag it out and make me wait. I'm just very neurotic about waiting."

"I'll let you know as soon as we've tried out the other candidates," I say.

"Who's your next candidate? Anybody I know?"

"A guy waiting for us over at Lake Actumber," I say.

"What's his name?" she asks.

"Goon."

Rachel nods. "Ah. Goon. Right. And then after that you're going to see Geek and Goober, right?"

"No, that really is his name," I say. "Tim Goon. His dad's got a place on Lake Actumber."

"That's a weird thing to name a lake after," she says.

Deshutsis's ears prick up.

"You, uh, have some direct experience with actumber?" he says.

She looks at him oddly. "I won a plate of it once, if that's what you mean."

Deshutsis nods. I look over at Beaterson, and he gives me a nod. This is classic Deshutsis.

"Interesting," Deshutsis says. "What did you do with it after you won it?"

"Do with it?" Rachel says, smiling.

"I mean—a whole plate of actumber . . ."

"I shared it with my friends," she says. "Well, I'd better get going, I see most of the team's here now. You have my cell-phone number, right, Flint?"

"Right."

She thanks us for giving her the tryout and turns to go.

"Hold it," Deshutsis says. "H-How did you win it?"

"What?"

"The actumber."

"It was at a county fair. There was this big walk-in freezer, and they had this swinging beef."

"Swinging beef?"

"Yeah, the display was called 'Side of Swingin' Beef.' And you were supposed to go in and guess how much the side of swingin' beef would weigh. So I wrote down four hundred and eleven pounds, and later that day they announced the actual weight. I didn't win, but I came in second and won the consolation prize, which was the plate of actumber."

Deshutsis's face is turning pink.

"Now, wait a minute—"

"What?"

"You expect me to believe that?"

"What?"

"There's no such thing as actumber!" Deshutsis says. "There is no such thing. Admit it."

Summerfield looks at him like he's lost it. "You—you're joking, right?"

"There's no such thing. I would have heard of it."

"Look, I have to get going. I just hope this whole tryout hasn't been a joke." She glances over at me now, not sure whether to smile or be offended.

"He's serious," I say. "We've never heard of actumber. None of us. Only it drives him crazier than it does us."

Deshutsis is shaking his head back and forth. "There is no such thing."

"Well, of course there's such a thing," she says with a laugh.

"Ten bucks," Deshutsis says. "I'll bet you ten bucks there's nothing in the English language called an actumber. I'll bet you can't even give me the definition."

"I don't want to take your money," Rachel says. "How about if I just tell you what it means, no charge." And here she is looking smack into Deshutsis's eyes. It looks like the Hungarian Method is being employed here, but I can't tell who's employing it on whom.

"All right," he says. "I'll call your bluff. Tell me."

"Make it a dollar," she says. "It'll cost you a dollar to find out what it means."

They shake hands on the bet.

"Actumber," she says. "A plate of fresh food made up of avocado, grapes, and meat paté. A sampler, of sorts."

"Prove it," says Deshutsis.

"Prove it! What do you mean, I just gave you the definition. Pay up. I want my dollar."

"You made that up out of thin air."

"I did not. The burden of proof is on you," she says. "The bet was whether or not I knew the definition and could provide it. I did. We weren't betting on whether I could furnish proof. If you want to challenge my definition, go ahead, but I'm right. So give me my dollar."

She holds out her hand.

Deshutsis opens his mouth. "I . . . left my wallet in the car."

"Now, why would you go and do that?" Rachel says.

"Here," I say. I've got some quarters in the back pocket of my sweats. I always have them for phone calls. I fish out four and hand them over to her.

"Thanks," she says.

I look down at her shorts and notice that they don't have any pockets. But there's a small pocket on the front of her rugby shirt, and she drops the quarters in.

"Don't get hurt out there today," I say, meeting her eyes. They are a deep, dark brown.

"I'll try not to," she says, meeting mine back.

Beaterson, Deshutsis, and I stand and watch her walk across the field and join her teammates.

15

"*What a shrew,*" Deshutsis says.

"Those bushes," Beaterson says.

"Furry," Deshutsis says. "It's like she's walking on a pair of shrubs."

"It gave me a chill," Beaterson says. "The hair stood up on the back of my neck."

We're back in Beaterson's LeSabre. I'm riding up front.

We left the rugby field a while ago, deciding not to wait around for the rugby match to start. I wouldn't have minded watching a little rugby and seeing if Summerfield got some action—I mean, after all, we have three hours to kill before we're meeting Goon—but Beaterson and Deshutsis said that watching women play rugby is too much like watching women play soccer, except in rugby they can pick up the ball and run with it and get tackled by the other women, and they cry a lot. I didn't see why this was a reason for not sticking around, but I didn't want to argue with them.

And besides, I think we all want to deliberate on Summerfield, and it would be better to do that without her being able to see us.

"She was so god-awful belligerent," Deshutsis says.

"And that dream thing," Beaterson says. "What was with that?"

"I didn't get that dream thing, either," Deshutsis says. "That was so off-the-wall it was spooky. Did you get that, Flint?"

"I think she was just trying to make conversation," I say.

"I don't think there's anything simpleminded about that one," Deshutsis says. "Did you notice how she used the word *utilize* instead of *use*?"

"I caught that," Beaterson says.

"She's on some kind of a mission," Deshutsis says. "She's got some kind of emasculation agenda."

"She's a ball-buster, all right," Beaterson says.

The mist of this morning is turning to rain, but Beaterson hasn't turned on his wipers yet, and it's almost impossible to see out his windshield.

We've just seen one of the best four-man flag-football players we'll ever hope to see, and these guys are ripping into her. Why? They are scared to death of her. They feel threatened by somebody who's that good, who's female, and who is capable of taking us to the next level, so long as we give her total equality.

I know exactly how they feel, because I feel it, too.

"You want to cross her off the list, then?" I say.

"Unless we have a strong desire to be henpecked to death," Deshutsis says.

"She just wants to show us up," Beaterson says. "She's got an agenda."

"Do you like her?" I ask.

"As a person?" Beaterson says, as if this is an odd question. "I've always thought she's okay."

"I like her," I say. "I like everything about her."

"Oh, I think we've always liked her well enough," Deshutsis says.

"She's very likable," Beaterson says. "She's fast, too. I'll give her that. She's a speedster. And she's got some moves. And she's not bad to look at, except for . . . "

"How about you, Flint?" Deshutsis says. "You want to start taking turns at quarterback? You want to start trading positions around in the name of fairness and equality? You want her to start calling plays, running the whole show? Is winning really worth that? Do we really want to win so bad that we're willing to give up control of our team?"

What he's saying is true, and it's sad. It's probably the main reason why we've hung on to Savage all this time without looking for a fifth man to add to our roster.

The subservience factor. We like having somebody who'll hike the ball every down, do whatever we tell him, and not be a threat to our pride and egos.

It's true, too, that whether or not we were able to get along with Summerfield and adjust to her, she would change us; she would change the chemistry between us three Clams. I don't know whether that would be bad or good, but it would be different.

"Well?" Deshutsis says to me. "What do you say? You going to tell us what you're thinking?"

"We don't need to decide anything until we see Goon," I say.

"Fair enough. Anything else?" he says.

"Yeah," I say. "You owe me a dollar."

Ever since we've had our driver's licenses, one of our favorite destinations, when we have some time to kill, is the big Goodwill store on Dearborn Street. You never know what kind of interesting discovery you might make there. Since the rugby fields are down in that part of town, we decide to take a side trip over to the Goodwill before we get some lunch.

The Goodwill is also one of the few places in Seattle where Beaterson's big old car isn't an abnormality. There are lots of big old cars parked in the parking lot, and others being driven around and around by drivers determined to find a parking place close to the entrance.

Beaterson parks in the farthest corner, and we head across the parking lot, past the espresso stand on the front sidewalk, and enter through the nonelectric glass doors into the ripe, musty, spinster's attic smells of old clothes, wigs, shoes, purses, old people, and fresh popcorn.

Deshutsis always lingers at the "Collectibles" to gaze at antique necklaces, hand-painted thimbles, ornamented tapestries, mink stoles, gramophones, music boxes, and porcelain Victorian figurines.

Beaterson nudges me with his elbow and whispers, "Womanly tendencies."

We leave Deshutsis behind and wander past the books and magazines, detouring down aisles of dead computer monitors, musical instruments, electric shavers, motherboards, office supplies.

TVs, radios, tapedecks.

Adding machines. Manual and electric type-writers.

A big sign in red letters tells you that all items are wysiwyg: "what you see is what you get."

Rachel Summerfield, I believe, is wysiwyg, too.

There's a long line of gleaming toasters, toaster ovens, an overhead projector without a light bulb, a bin full of cameras.

And just before I head over to the sporting goods and ski stuff, something catches my eye. Something smooth and white and marbly, hidden amid the toasters.

A giant pearl. A full moon, with one thin yellow stripe running around it like the equator.

It's a bowling ball.

What's a bowling ball doing in the toaster section? Sometimes that's the way it is at the Goodwill; things get picked up in one place and put down in another, usually by accident.

I pick it up off the shelf and cradle it, rotating and inspecting it for a chunk missing or a crack. But, except for a few scratches and one tiny nick, it seems perfect.

I figure it's about twelve pounds. I heft it and bounce it up and down in my cupped palms, as if it's somebody's severed head.

Now for the really big moment: I slide my two right-hand middle fingers and thumb into its three holes. The crowd in my head is chanting, "Fit! Fit!"

It's a perfect fit. My fingers are home. Home! Not even realizing it, I say the word out loud, "Home. Home."

Beaterson and Deshutsis crack up. I hadn't meant for them to hear it.

"Home, home?" Deshutsis says.

They crack up some more.

It will become one of the thousand private jokes we've collected over our lives. The time we were at Goodwill and Flint put his fingers in the bowling ball and said "Home, home." Months from now they'll use it on me at some appropriate but unexpected moment.

You can imagine what would happen if they knew about Savage being stuck in the creek bed with Kat Olney. The private joke to end all private jokes.

But I feel like I've hit the jackpot. A bowling ball. Here is some luck!

The previous owner's name is engraved on the ball in blue letters the size of fingernail clippings: *Proud Jerry.*

How often do you find something in almost perfect shape, a perfect fit, especially among all the rejects?

Suddenly, I remember something. This morning when I was throwing footballs to Rachel Summerfield, I threw her one out of her reach, and she dove for it. She actually left her feet and flew headlong with her arms outstretched.

On our way to the checkout counter, something stops Beaterson in his tracks: a squished cowboy hat. He puts down the funnel and two-inch drill bit that he had intended to buy, picks up the hat, punches it into shape, and tries it on. It looks like the real thing.

"I wouldn't put that on my head," Deshutsis says. "No telling where that thing has been."

"Out in the wind and weather and dust and sagebrush," Beaterson says in a cowboy drawl, squinting his eyes. Give him a Marlboro and a mustache, and he'd look just right on a billboard.

"Since when have you become a redneck?" Deshutsis says.

"A cowboy hat keeps you shady under the sun and dry under the rain," Beaterson drawls.

"Do the words *hick* and *hayseed* mean anything to you?" Deshutsis says.

Beaterson looks at me. "What do you think, Captain?"

"How much is it?" I say.

"I don't reckon that matters," he says. "This here's a Stetson, can you believe that?"

"Are you going to use the phony drawl every time you put on the hat?" I say.

"May-be."

"It is pretty redneck," I say.

"Well, son, maybe I'm born to be a redneck."

I notice the price tag. It's twenty dollars *more* than my bowling ball!

Beaterson checks the cash situation in his wallet, and leaves the funnel and drill bit behind. And keeps the Stetson.

As we get near the counter, Beaterson and Deshutsis are razzing me because I wasn't able to find a bag— a chalise—to carry the ball in. Usually they have half a dozen bowling bags in the sporting goods department, but today there isn't a single one.

"Better keep an eye on that ball or it'll roll away on you!"

"Put a leash on it and you can drag it."

"Carry it in a shopping bag."

"What are you going to call your pet bowling ball? Cotton Puff?"

"How about Milk Eye?"

"Pearlie?"

"Marshmallow?"

I let Beaterson check out first with his hat. When it's my turn, as the cashier is ringing me up, I think of one of the names I just heard: "Milk Eye." It reminds me of something. An image comes to mind: Glen Como's eye, one milky-white eye, going up into his head.

"Sir?"

The cashier is looking at me.

She has dark brown skin, her head is wrapped in a shawl, and her eyes are very bright.

"Are you all right?" she says in a thick accent.

It takes me a moment to remember where I am. I nod. "Yeah. Just making sure I really want to buy this."

I dig out my wallet and hand her a twenty.

16

"*I suppose* you're going to want to try old Pearlie out tonight," Beaterson says, putting on his cowboy hat when we get outside.

"I like the sound of that," I say.

Deshutsis comes hurrying up behind us. He had lagged behind to examine the headlines of the Saturday morning newspapers in the coin-op dispensers. He wants people who shop at Goodwill to think he's up on current events.

"I guess that means we're definitely not going to Savage's party," Deshutsis says. "That's fine with me. I'd rather win some money off you two. Nickel a pin. I'll clean up. Whoo-hoo."

"This ball is going to bring me luck," I say. "This is my lucky ball. I'd rather have luck than wisdom."

"You really mean that?" Beaterson says.

"I think wisdom is overrated," I say. "There's nothing more fun than a run of good luck."

As I climb into the LeSabre's backseat and put my bowling ball beside me like a special passenger, I feel another wave of happiness, like the one I felt back at the rugby field. I don't know where it's coming from. The thought of killing time on this Saturday morning, grabbing lunch somewhere, going bowling later tonight with my new bowling ball—it just makes me happy. But I suppose I ought to be stressed out. I'm seeing Cade Savage tomorrow and I don't know what I'm going to say to him. We have to have a fourth guy by tomorrow evening, and we're not making any progress. We haven't played a single practice game yet. I'm an orphan while my parents are in Alaska. We haven't made our visit to Glen Como's grave. Rachel Summerfield will be expecting me to call her today.

It's a mess, really. And I don't see any way out.

Beaterson is able to wear his cowboy hat inside his car. We're heading west on Dearborn, under the big green Jose Rizal Bridge. Straight ahead is Safeco Field and the new Seahawks football stadium, which is where the old Kingdome used to be. Beyond that is the waterfront, and Puget Sound. To the right is the International District, and that's where we're going. Beaterson and Deshutsis are arguing about whether we should have dim sum for lunch. I know I'm probably going to have to cast the tie-breaking vote.

Beaterson cashed his paycheck yesterday after school,

and he is in favor of dim sum. He works for Kvorcek's Meats, in the meat freezers. Talk about sides of swingin' beef—Beaterson knows swingin' beef. He makes twice more an hour than I do at my warehouse job at Skipper Luggage. He says he can get me hired on, but I don't want to work at Kvorcek's, not even for twice the money. Beaterson has told me what it's like to work there. How there's a pecking order, and how the old-timers give you shit all day, and you constantly have to prove how much of a man you are. It's all one big pissing contest. I know I'd probably last about a day. What gives Beaterson an advantage there among those hard-living and hard-fighting men? They're exactly like his father.

Deshutsis, who has never had a job aside from mowing lawns, is arguing against dim sum. He says it misfires in his stomach.

Beaterson stops at a crosswalk where two Japanese tourist teenagers in white skirts, white sweaters, and white sneakers are waiting to cross. He signals them to go ahead.

"Take your time, ladies, and let us enjoy the view," he says in his new cowboy drawl.

The girls glance at Beaterson and giggle and say something to each other. Beaterson tips his hat, and they hurry even faster.

"They must think you're Tom Cruise," Deshutsis says dryly.

"Aw, can it," Beaterson says.

Beaterson stays at the crosswalk as another female pedestrian comes along. This one is Caucasian and dressed in a business suit. We eyeball her as she crosses in front of us. She's got a nice body and nice hair—she obviously invests a lot of time and money in self-maintenance—but her face is kind of homely.

Beaterson leans partway out his window and says in his most sincere voice, "You sure do have a beautiful body."

The lady just turns and gives us a bored look, and slowly shakes her head back and forth.

For a moment we are all speechless.

There's a loud honk from behind. Beaterson starts, then recovers. Slowly, he turns around and sticks his head out the window, cowboy hat and all, and yells, "Lick my exhaust pipe!"

I'm afraid to see who the driver is. It could be a lone, gun-toting psycho, or a carload of hungry longshoremen on their lunch break.

I turn around and look. It's a soccer mom in a minivan with a load of boys who are—surprise—wearing soccer uniforms.

"Last time I had dim sum," Deshutsis says, "I had a really explosive toilet experience."

Beaterson and I thank him for sharing that.

I turn around and take another look at the lady in the minivan. She's afraid to honk again.

I turn back around and face front. "I'm going to vote no on the dim sum," I say.

Deshutsis actually comes up with a pretty good suggestion: hot dogs. Not just any hot dog; one of those Chicago-style kielbasas that are so good they snap when you bite into them and actually squirt juice all over.

We're driving by the old Rainier Brewery, which is now owned by Tully's Coffee. They took the big Rainier *R* down and put up a green *T* for Tully's. Another Seattle landmark gone, relegated to the Museum of History and Industry over on Montlake.

I lean forward and look at Deshutsis. "Tell me Tim Goon will be the answer to all our problems."

"Tim Goon will be the answer to all our problems."

"You don't sound very convincing."

"Well, I suppose that depends on how you define *answer* and how you define *problems*."

"You sounded pretty sure of him last night," I say. "You called him the Goon Solution. Does he have any talent or not?"

"As I've pointed out many times, I haven't seen him in action, but going on my gut, I'd have to say that's an affirmative."

"Is that your gut before or after your explosive toilet experience?" Beaterson says.

We're looking for a particular kielbasa place, but we can't seem to find it. After going around in circles for a half hour, we give up, and end up heading northbound on the Alaskan Way Viaduct, with Puget Sound all spread out on our left and downtown Seattle on our right. This viaduct has one of the best views in the city.

We go through the Battery Street tunnel and cross the Aurora Bridge. We are starting to get irritable with hunger. Passing by Woodland Park and Greenlake, we notice a girl on our left, wearing funky wingtip glasses, driving an old Datsun pickup. She's got a big, friendly-looking dog in the front seat beside her.

"Not bad," Beaterson says.

"Mousy," Deshutsis says.

Her dog is grinning at us, wanting to make friends—probably needs a male figure in his life.

"She reminds me of some actress, only with glasses," Beaterson says.

"Is that what you'd say to her while applying the Hungarian Method?" Deshutsis says.

Beaterson stays in the right-hand lane as the girl speeds up and drives out of our lives.

I look at my bowling ball. I want to believe in good luck. Can there ever be such a thing as a perfect fit? Proud Jerry. I wonder what kind of man Proud Jerry was. Proud, I suppose. And dead. He's got to be dead. Bowling balls don't end up at Goodwill unless . . .

It can mean only one thing: Proud Jerry is dead and his heirs do not bowl.

Deshutsis suddenly jerks forward and slaps the dashboard, which startles Beaterson.

"I've got it!"

"Jesus! Don't make sudden movements like that!"

"Sorry. Take a right up here."

"Where?"

"Home Depot. They have great hot dogs."

"What?"

"Trust me. Turn here!"

Beaterson steps on the brake and cranks the wheel to the right, and the car plunges down a steep incline into the parking lot of the Home Depot.

"These hot dogs better be good," Beaterson says.

"Define *good*," Deshutsis says.

17

Home Depot's hopping on this rainy noon-day Saturday. Home, home—Home Depot.

I smell hot dogs.

The snack kiosk is outside the store on the sidewalk. It's a zipped-up heated pouch. Working behind the counter is a lone skinny girl, her wispy hair dyed in various colors. She's cute, in a birdlike way. We turn on our charm.

"How're the dogs?" Beaterson says. He's still wearing his cowboy hat.

She seems confused as to how to handle us. Or maybe it's not confusion; maybe it's caution at being alone in a zip-lock pouch with three guys her own age whose collective charm has just been activated.

"Do these dogs snap when you bite them?" Beaterson says.

"What?"

"I want to know if they squirt juice on the windshield when you sink your teeth into them," Beaterson says.

The girl looks around for help, but there is none. I don't think she gets paid enough to deal with people like us.

Deshutsis is studying the "Question of the Day," which is on the chalkboard next to the counter.

Correctly answer the "Question of the Day" and receive 10% off your purchase.

Written in cursive on the smeared chalkboard is the following:

What was the name of the play that President Abraham Lincoln was watching when he was assassinated?

I look at Deshutsis. He is staring wide-eyed at the chalkboard. I catch a whiff of English Leather coming from him.

"It was Yankee something," he says to himself. "Yankee Peddlar. Yankee Doodle in the . . ."

"Nobody's got it yet today," the girl says, leaning forward on her skinny arms and admiring the question, then running her eyes up and down Deshutsis's tanned, aristocratic profile and apparently admiring that, too. I experience a twinge of envy.

"You get that right and I will personally take this hat off to you," Beaterson says.

Deshutsis wets his lips and doesn't blink for many seconds.

I tell Beaterson I think I'll pass on these so-called Polish dogs.

Beaterson nods in agreement. "Kielbasa these ain't," he says.

"You ought to give them a chance," the girl says, glancing from Beaterson to me.

"My tastebuds don't believe in taking chances," I say.

I walk out onto the front sidewalk. Beaterson and Deshutsis are still inside. I don't mind standing hungry in the rain, watching the people come and go from the store's entrance and exit.

An elderly man in baggy khaki work pants emerges from the store's exit, and I realize it's, of all people, my barber, Bob Miller. He's pushing a shopping cart containing a stack of fertilizer bags and some rebar. He glances at me, recognizes me, and frowns, which is about the only expression you'll ever get from Bob, even when he's glad to see you.

"Not cutting hair today?" I say.

"I'm too damn old to cut hair on Saturday," he says.

He asks how my parents are doing, and I tell him they're on a cruise. Bob must be seventy years old. He cut my dad's hair when my dad was a kid. I help him load his stuff into the back of his truck. His Pekingese is barking at me. Before I can blink, Bob's in his truck and practically backing over me. As he drives away, he tells me to stop by for a haircut one of these days. I say I'll do that.

Beaterson has come out and is standing on the sidewalk. He doesn't have a hot dog. I go over to him.

"This was a mistake," he says.

"Why is everything such a big decision for us?" I say.

"Wasn't that your barber?"

"Yes."

Deshutsis comes out and wanders over to us, looking dazed. "I know it," he says, shaking his head. "It's right on the tip of my tongue."

"Either you know it or you don't," Beaterson says.

"I've just momentarily forgotten it. I'm in the retrieval mode."

"Then, you don't know it. It's more accurate to say 'I used to know it.'" Beaterson seems pleased with his display of logic.

Deshutsis rubs his chin. Abe Lincoln is his main man. Lincoln, Lee, Ulysses S. Grant, all those Civil War guys and Founding Fathers. He is quite up on them.

"It had the word *National* in it, I think," he says lamely.

"*National Velvet*," Beaterson says. "*National Hot Tin Roof. National Malibu Barbie.*"

"Something like *National Holiday*," Deshutsis says. "*National Sons and Daughters.*"

"Let's go to Zesto's and get some burgers," I say. "It's not too far from here."

"I can't believe how stupid I am," Deshutsis says as we're heading for Beaterson's car.

"Let go of it, Mr. Actumber." Beaterson digs for his keys.

"Wait a minute." Deshutsis's eyes light up. "I have an idea."

"I'm afraid," Beaterson says.

"Let me just walk over to that far fence, way over there. You guys wait for me at the car. If I can't remember it in that period of time, I'll go back and ask the girl for the answer. Deal?"

Beaterson and I agree to this. While Professor Deshutsis wanders over toward the fence, hands behind his back, Beaterson and I get the football and start playing catch.

"Running into my barber is a good omen," I say.

"Why's that?"

"I don't know," I say. "It's the weekend before the start of flag-football season, and we're playing catch in the parking lot of Home Depot. I don't think it can get any worse than this."

"It's all Savage's fault," Beaterson says.

I suppose Beaterson is right. Savage knows it's all his fault, too. He figures everything is his fault, including Glen Como being dead. He thinks everybody holds him responsible for that, and he feels guilty, and he figures we wish that he could trade places with Glen.

And I suppose the sad, brutal truth is that he's right. He did sort of indirectly kill Glen Como, and there's probably no one in the entire world, other than maybe Cade's parents (and even that's debatable), who wouldn't have preferred that Glen had fallen on top of Cade instead of the other way around, and that it would be Cade Savage's grave we'd visit instead of Glen's.

That's a terrible thought, I know. That's why we try not to think it very often. I'll bet Cade tries not to think about it, too. In fact, I'll bet he tries every way he can to forget it.

I toss a long one to Beaterson and he bobbles it but holds on. He'll drop an occasional pass or two, but he's got good hands for a guy with his bulk. He would have been a sensational middle linebacker. Strong, quick, savvy. Tough. Fearless.

"You remember what you said last night about the angel?" I say, walking toward him.

"Yeah?"

"Maybe an angel really did come. What she gave you was a thought in your head that disturbed you. Maybe she was telling you to go and *get* a football scholarship. It's not too late for you, you know."

Beaterson grips the football for a moment, giving me a look. Then he tosses it to me.

"I'm not sure I follow what you're saying," he says.

"I think you do," I say, catching the ball. "Give it some thought. Run it by your sister."

He takes his hat off and looks inside it, then puts it back on.

Deshutsis has turned around and is coming back toward us. I know that look on his face. I know it from a couple hundred hours of poker games with him. When he's sitting on a good hand, he can bluff Beaterson and he can bluff Savage, but he can't bluff me. Right now, if he were a dog, his tail would be wagging.

"He knows it," I say.

Beaterson and I follow him back to the hot dog kiosk. I'm holding the football under my arm.

The girl's face brightens at the sight of Deshutsis. She barely glances at Beaterson and me.

Deshutsis orders a hot dog. Polish. Nothing to drink.

"That'll be $3.18."

"I'll take a shot at the trivia question."

"Okay, if you get it right, you get ten percent off. That would be thirty-one cents off. That would make your total $2.87."

Deshutsis smiles and seems to grow an inch or two. "The answer is *Our American Cousin*."

The girl beams.

"You're the"—she gulps—"first one today who's gotten it. Ten percent off!"

For the second time, I envy Deshutsis. Triumph is a sweet thing. And there was no luck involved. Maybe that casts doubt on my theory about luck being preferable to wisdom.

Beaterson and I each shake his hand, and Beaterson tips his hat first to Deshutsis, then to the girl.

By the time we get to Beaterson's car, the hot dog is gone and Deshutsis is wiping his mouth with a napkin.

"We had a feeling you'd do it," Beaterson says. He sounds proud.

"That's right," I say. "We had faith in you. Not much, but some."

"It came to me when I grabbed the fence," Deshutsis says. "Right up until the second I grabbed the fence, I didn't have it. Making contact with the fence helped jar something in me. Suddenly, I went from not knowing to knowing. Life is good."

"How was the dog?"

"The dog was okay."

We head back down Aurora and then cut west over Phinny Ridge, toward Ballard and Zesto's. Deshutsis burps resonantly. The smell of mustard and wiener wafts back to me. No onions.

"You know how it came to me?" Deshutsis says.

"Yeah," Beaterson says. "You touched the fence."

"It came in a flash. You know, when something pops

into your mind—just, *pop!*—it gives you a pretty good idea of what it's like to be a genius."

Deshutsis is preening. He's hot.

"Lincoln is my man!" he says. "Ling cone! Mah man!"

"Shut up," Beaterson says.

18

Lake Actumber is a good thirty miles north of
Seattle, past Lynnwood. It's a small private lake encircled
by houses, most of them one-story ramblers with back-
yards that slope down to it. One section of the lake has a
cluster of three-story apartment houses, and in one of
those is where Goon's dad lives.

We find Goon down by the dock, working on his
jet ski.

His dad is with him, and we all shake hands. Goon's
dad is young-looking, with salt-and-peppery flattened-
down hair. He seems like a soft-spoken, friendly, socially
awkward man, and I get the feeling he's more comfortable
around people our age than those in his own age group.
He reminds me of a middle-school teacher, or maybe
a driver's-ed teacher. He has a pasty complexion that is
pocked with acne scars from when he was our age.

Tim Goon is wearing a tank top the same color as
the stripe around my bowling ball.

Goon's dad nods at the football in my hands. "Going to play some football?"

"Yeah, we're getting ready for flag-football season next week," I say. "We play in a four-on-four league."

"They're looking for another guy to join their team," Goon says.

Mr. Goon brightens. "Oh, really?" His eyebrows go up, and he seems delighted at what he's just heard, and that we've come all this way to recruit his son. He seems interested in the flag-football league, the rules and procedures, and asks several questions that are slightly more knowledgeable than ones you'd get from the average person. I do most of the talking, with Beaterson and Deshutsis tossing in their two cents.

"Would you guys like a cold can of pop?" Mr. Goon asks.

Beaterson and I say that would be great. Deshutsis asks if there's any cream soda. Mr. Goon says no, no cream soda. Deshutsis says, how about root beer. Mr. Goon says he might have a can of root beer. "A&W?" Deshutsis says. Mr. Goon chuckles and nods as he's walking away; I don't think he heard what Deshutsis said.

We stand around watching Tim Goon work on his jet ski. His big hands are covered with grime. The grit has gotten underneath his fingernails. Engine parts are strewn everywhere like wreckage.

Beaterson and Goon launch into mechanic's talk. Symptoms and diagnoses are discussed. Terms are tossed back and forth. Intake plate. Crank case. Shavings in the carburetor. Carburetor arm.

Mr. Goon comes back carrying four cans of generic cola.

"Sorry, I guess I was out of root beer," he says.

"Oh." To Deshutsis, generic brands of anything are white trash. He puts the unopened can down on the grass.

Tim Goon takes a long, manly guzzle of his pop, then wipes his mouth with the back of his greasy hand.

"Did you try draining the crank case, Tim?" Mr. Goon says.

More mechanic talk. I turn and look at the small dark lake. I try to imagine skinny-dipping in this lake with some skinny girls. It would have to be at night, of course. That's obvious, with all these houses around. Strange, skinny-dipping is something I've always imagined doing at dusk, not in the pitch-dark.

"Well," Mr. Goon says after a while, "I'll just let you men do your work. You need anything, just holler. I'll be up at the apartment."

After his dad has left, I ask Tim, "Is it legal to run a jet ski on this lake?"

"For now," he says. "Some folks don't like it, but they haven't managed to get them banned yet."

I catch a strong whiff of BO from him that almost knocks me over.

"When was the last time you had it running?" I ask.

"Never. I bought it at a junk shop for twenty-five dollars."

"Figuring you could fix it?" I say.

"No," Deshutsis says. "He bought it so he could strip it apart and stare at the pieces."

"Do you snow ski?" I ask Tim, ignoring Deshutsis.

"Yeah, occasionally."

"Where do you go?"

"Here and there. How about you?"

"Stevens Pass, usually," I say. "Unless I can get down to Crystal. But Crystal's a long way to go just for the day. You pretty much have to stay overnight."

Goon nods. He finishes his can of cola, burps, and drops it on the ground. I look at Deshutsis, but he turns and gazes out across the lake. Some geese are sitting on the dock, and there is green poop all over it.

Beaterson, who's been tinkering with the engine all this time, stands up and goes down to the water and washes his hands in the lake.

"I don't know," he says. "I'm starting to think the whole carb's fried."

"It can't be," Goon says.

Still squatting, Beaterson turns around. "Do you have a cabin at Crystal Mountain?"

"What? No. Why do you ask?"

"Deshutsis told us you had a ski cabin at Crystal Mountain."

"I don't think I said that exactly," Deshutsis says. "I think you must have misunderstood me."

"Do you know why we came here today?" Beaterson says.

Goon looks a little confused. He looks from Beaterson to Deshutsis with a tentative grin.

In the corner of my eye, I notice Goon's dad has stepped out onto his balcony, which overlooks the lake. He's leaning on it, looking over at us from time to time but mostly just looking out at the lake.

Goon shrugs. "To hang out and help me with my jet ski?" Goon says. "And, I guess, give me a tryout for your football team."

"You mind if I toss you a few?" I say.

Goon laughs and shrugs.

"You'd better wipe your hands off," I say. "We don't want to get the football all greasy."

Goon picks up an oily rag and wipes his hands off, but they are still black.

I almost throw him the ball, but I stop. "Hey, Tim. I know I'm going to sound like a fussy old woman, but would you mind washing them?"

At this moment I don't like us very much—

especially myself. I *do* sound like a fussy old woman. I kind of like Goon. I like his dad, too, who is still standing out on the balcony, watching us. But I'm starting to feel depressed. Maybe it's partly because the sky is getting dark and it looks like it's going to start pouring in a minute. I think about my parents, somewhere up in Alaska.

Goon finishes washing his hands in the lake, and stands now with his big, veiny meat hooks dripping, and I can see the grit and grime under his fingernails.

I make sure he's ready, then toss him an easy pass. He sticks his paws straight out, partly to shield his face and partly to catch the ball, and the ball caroms off his forearm and wobbles on down the slope, rolling over the goose shit and into the lake.

"Raindrop got in my eye," Goon says, shaking his fingers.

"The football," Beaterson says, pointing.

Goon hustles down to the lake and tries to reach the ball, but it seems to have a little motor in it, and it keeps on going farther out.

"Damn raindrop got in my eye," Goon says.

"We heard you the first time," Beaterson says.

Beaterson finds a branch on the ground and uses it to try to reach the football, but it's not long enough.

Goon wades out into the lake. He is chest-high before he can retrieve the ball.

"It's warm," he says, and lets out a laugh that strikes me as borderline hysterical.

For the next five minutes I toss him passes, and he tries to catch them by clapping his hands together and averting his face. His pants are sopping wet, but even if they weren't it would still be hopeless; he might as well be trying to catch the ball wearing a sheet over his head and a pair of boxing gloves. He is beyond uncoordinated. There's some serious defect in his motor skills. He is a piece of defective merchandise. If he were an item at Goodwill, he'd be in the reject bin in the far northwest corner, beyond even the plumbing fixtures.

"Try hiking the ball, Tim," Deshutsis says. "We're mainly looking for someone to be the hiker."

"Sure. Okay."

He wipes the goose poop off the ball and turns around and hikes the ball between his legs, but he doesn't know when to let go of it, and it keeps slapping his rear end. I see his dad on the balcony, watching us. It must be painful for Mr. Goon to see this. He wants the best for his son, but he's powerless to help. I want to cry. I feel a sick feeling in the pit of my stomach, like the one you get on the first day of school, or when you see someone you like getting beaten in a fight.

I pick up the football and take it down to the water to wash it off. "We'd better get going," I say.

"What's the hurry?" Deshutsis says.

"There's no hurry," I say. "I guess I meant *I'd* better get going; you can stay if you want."

"But Tim's going to get his jet ski running," Deshutsis says. "I told him we'd pitch in and help."

"I have to go. I'd like to stay. This is a neat lake, but I have to get going."

"I don't know why my hands are so retarded today," Tim says. "They're usually not that bad."

"Thanks for letting us come over." I hold out my hand and we shake.

"I can practice hiking the ball," he says.

"We can't use you, Tim," I say.

Goon laughs. "What?"

"We can't use you."

"Oh."

"I hope you get that thing running," I say, smiling miserably.

Goon laughs again.

Beaterson says good-bye and shakes Goon's hand, and he and I walk up the slope, around the side of the apartment building. Mr. Goon is no longer standing out on the balcony. He has gone inside.

There's a thunderstorm passing.

Beaterson and I are watching it from inside his car, still parked in Mr. Goon's driveway. I guess we're waiting for Deshutsis.

Pretty soon, Deshutsis comes strolling around the corner as if it's a sunny day. He gets into the backseat. He's drenched.

"Don't say anything," he says. "Don't either of you say anything. Whatever you can possibly say, either one of you, don't bother, because I am always one step ahead of you and I know what you're going to say before you say it, and anything that you can possibly be thinking of saying right now, I know exactly what it is, so don't even bother saying it. There's no need to. I know what you are going to say, so you might as well just—"

"SHUT UP!" Beaterson screams. "SHUT. UP."

We sit in silence for a few minutes, watching and listening to the torrents of rain.

Pretty soon, the storm passes, and Beaterson sighs and looks at his watch.

"It's after four," he says. "What are we going to do?"

"Too early to go bowling," Deshutsis says. "Too early to grab a bite to eat. We could—"

"I'm not asking you," Beaterson says. His knuckles turn white as he holds the steering wheel.

"Maybe go back and play some pool," I say.

"I don't mean right now," Beaterson says. "I mean, what are we going to do with this team?"

I look over at my bowling ball. Proud Jerry. I reach out and touch it with my fingertips.

Beaterson puts his hand on the ignition to start the car, but halts himself.

"Look," he says. "We know the reality here. Either we dump Savage and go with Summerfield, or we stay with Savage. Those are our two choices."

"Those just aren't acceptable," Deshutsis says.

"Oh, well, thank you," Beaterson says. "Great. Now that we've solved that, we can relax and go bowling."

"You want reality, I'll give you reality," I say, stroking Proud Jerry.

"Please do," Deshutsis says with fake civility.

"We've tried out three different people this weekend," I say. "But we've just been going through the motions. There's no way we're going to dump Savage. He knows that. It's not that we don't have any other choice. We do. We could go with Summerfield. But we're not going to. Because she scares the hell out of us. She's a radical, and we're conservatives. This weekend, we've run away from pretty much everything new and different that's come along. And that's the reality, guys. We should just accept it. We're set in our ways. That's the way we are. We may not like it, but we're comfortable with it.

"So, here's what we're going to do. Tomorrow, after Cade's had his party, I'm going to go see him, as planned. I'm going to have a long talk with him. Not just about football, but we're going to talk about Glen, and how Cade feels about Glen's death, and whether Cade feels like the odd man out, and all kinds of stuff. When it's all over with, I don't know if Cade's going to feel any better about himself or life or anything else, but he'll be ready to play football."

Beaterson nods. I don't think it's a nod of agreement, just a nod of acceptance.

I look at Deshutsis in the backseat, drip-drying. He nods, too.

Beaterson starts the car, and reverses down the driveway to the main road. It's a busy road, all the worse because of the rain. He has to wait for a long time until there's an opening in traffic, then back out onto the road, shift into D, and accelerate.

"Oh, no," Deshutsis says.

Beaterson turns on his wipers.

"Aw, damn," Deshutsis says. He puts his hands up and buries his face.

A minute goes by.

"Damn, damn, damn."

"All right," Beaterson says. "What? What is it?"

Deshutsis just shakes his head.

"What is it?" I say.

Deshutsis sits there shaking his head. Finally, he removes his hands from his face.

"I cannot even believe it," he says.

"What?" I say.

"I forgot to ask his dad what *actumber* means."

19

Hard to believe, but for the past three hours I don't think we've said more than a dozen words. We stopped for some cheeseburgers and ended up back at Deshutsis's apartments, playing pool in the cabana. Now it's seven-thirty, and we're at the Sundowner Bowl, in the Lake City area.

A while ago I checked my home answering machine for messages, and there was one from Summerfield. She was calling to tell me that she'd be home all evening, and that I can call her cell phone anytime.

I haven't called her yet. What am I supposed to tell her? That even though she's one of the best flag-football players we've ever seen, she just isn't right for us? She just doesn't fit?

And right now Cade Savage's party is probably starting up. What will I say to him tomorrow, when he's all hung over? That even though he's a shrimp and a loser, and against our better judgment, we're going to keep him because he's our friend and we don't want to see him throw his life away?

The bowling alley is pretty quiet. It will probably pick up around nine, but it never gets as hectic here as at Robin Hood Lanes. Bill, who works behind the counter, greets us. His belly is huge and he has a tired pale face and dark circles under his eyes, and he's usually got a cigarette poking out from the corner of his mouth. He's not a great poster child for bowling.

He gives us our favorite lane, number 32, the farthest on the end.

"I got a new ball," I tell him while he's placing our rental shoes on the counter.

"Let's have a look." He inspects it, holding the cigarette between his lips, squinting through the smoke. "Proud Jerry, huh? How much you pay for old Proud Jerry?"

"Twelve."

"Dollars?"

"No, drachmas."

"Hmm. Little banged up. Drill holes look a little odd. But I guess he don't look too bad."

Banged up? What's he talking about?

Being a ball owner, I now have the unhurried luxury of putting on my shoes at lane 32 while Beaterson and Deshutsis have to go hunting for the balls they want.

I take a couple of practice rolls, concentrating on my form. I am enamored with watching my white ball with the yellow stripe. I am so enamored that I don't hit the pocket or knock down many pins, but that's all right, I have to find my rhythm.

I wiggle my fingers. They feel all right. I wonder if I should have cleaned out the inside of the drill holes, maybe gunk or jelly or something gathers in there and you should clean it out.

We start our first game.

"Snow White!" Beaterson and Deshutsis call. "Cotton Puff! Tie a yellow ribbon round the snowball! Pearl-o-the-Oyster! Moon Ball!"

I do the best I can to block them out, but my first several frames are disappointing. In fact, not until the fifth frame do I even get my first spare. In the seventh frame, I roll a strike. I do the Glen Como Kick, named after Glen Como, who, upon rolling a strike, would leap into the air, clicking his heels together in midair while at the same time grabbing his head with his hands and twisting it sideways. It's a lot of work. But Glen didn't have to do it very often, because he hardly ever got a strike.

My thumb is throbbing. There's a wicked black slash at the base of my thumb. A gouge. A crevasse. It is so deep it looks like a permanent indentation.

My thumb starts swelling up.

What kind of weird thumb did Proud Jerry have, anyway?

What kind of a freak was he?

I tell myself I just have to get used to the ball.

Electric jolts of pain shoot up from my thumb to everywhere.

Deshutsis wins the first game with a higher than average 183. Beaterson comes in second with a very respectable 171. I come in last with a feeble 131. At a nickel a pin, I hate to think about how much money I'm down after the first game. Better to think that there are two more games to go and I will stage a comeback.

The question is, should I hang on to this ball out of loyalty and stubborn pride, thereby doing permanent damage to my right hand, my *throwing* hand, for God's sake? Or should I cut my losses, swallow my pride, save my thumb, and admit that this ball is a dog? There's a nice moral dilemma for you. Ah, home, home. No such place. No such thing as a perfect fit. I should have known.

So much for the theory that seeing my barber would be a good omen.

"This ball is unusable," I say to Beaterson and Deshutsis. "The drills are weird; they're killing my thumb."

Beaterson and Deshutsis examine my thumb in grave silence.

Beaterson makes a face. "Man. You'd better hold that under some running water. Go find another ball."

"Wait a minute, is that allowed?" Deshutsis says.

"What do you mean, is that allowed?" Beaterson says.

"Well, I mean, I'm ahead in the first game. I'm not sure it's exactly kosher to change horses in the middle of the race or to change balls in the middle of the bowling contest."

Beaterson looks at him. "Are you joking or are you totally sick? His thumb's falling off."

"I could lodge a protest, you know," Deshutsis says.

"But you won't," Beaterson says.

I leave Proud Jerry on the ball return and go off to look for a replacement. I find number 3080, an old familiar friend, all gouged and nicked up like the ears of a tomcat.

The second game, Deshutsis is superhot. This time he ends up with a 192. Beaterson comes in with a 155. I end up with a 114.

I don't want to do the math.

In the empty rest room, I scream silently and thrash around to get rid of some of my rage. I hate to lose. I hate it, hate it, hate it.

I recover my composure and go out to face Deshutsis and the third game. It's his night. When he gets a strike, he does a little victory dance and says, "That was for Lincoln! Yeah! My man Lincoln! *Whooo! American Cousin!* Oh, yeah, bayyyyy bee!"

To make matters worse, during our third game, three really obnoxious post–high school couples take the lane next to us—loud smooching, nonstop smoking, one guy with a hacking cough; they are total lowlifes.

We finish the third and final game: Deshutsis 188, Beaterson 150, Me 120.

Deshutsis hums while he perkily calculates the grand totals: Deshutsis 563, Beaterson 476, Me 365.

"Well, here's the bad news, guys. Beaterson owes me $4.35. And McCallister, you owe me—*ouch!*—$9.90. Oh, yeah, pony up, baby!"

I have this fantasy of slamming my white bowling ball down on Deshutsis's head and hearing his head crack open.

Actually, for a long time, I've wanted to do an experiment. What would happen to a bowling ball if you dropped it onto cement from, say, ten feet? Would it break into one or two or several pieces, or would it bounce? It seems very solid; I'm not even sure what a bowling ball is made of. But tonight I'm going to find out once and for all.

20

The sky has cleared and there's a full moon out. It's around ten o'clock. We stopped for more cheeseburgers and fries and are now back in Beaterson's car.

Deshutsis is sitting in the front passenger seat. All that money he won off us has made him giddy. The three of us love to win, there's no doubt about that. We love to win, and we hate to lose. That's another reason why we make such a good team.

But he's a little too cheerful. He's singing an incredibly irritating song he made up while we were waiting at the drive-through for our cheeseburgers:

All I wan-na do is beat you
All I wan-na do is defeat you.

"Please," Beaterson says. "Please."
"Sorry," Deshutsis says. "I can't seem to help it."
"Try a little harder," Beaterson says.

Deshutsis has apparently fallen under the spell of his own singing voice. It's happened to all of us before. You get hooked on a certain song, and you can't stop.

All I wan-na do is ace you
All I wan-na do is disgrace you.

Beaterson, not looking at him, says in a quiet, teeth-clenched voice, "Okay. I'm asking you real nice for the fifth time. Will you stop that. Pretty please."

There is a tremble to his voice. Not a good sign.

"There is no one who hates losing as much as I do," Deshutsis says. "And even more so when money is involved. But when it's over, it's over. Get over it, Beater-wipe."

Beaterson doesn't say anything.

I told Beaterson and Deshutsis what I would like to do with Proud Jerry, and they seemed very interested. In fact, Beaterson said he knows of an old road with an overpass where I can drop the ball down onto the road, and I know exactly where he's talking about, and that's where we're going—we'll see if the bowling ball breaks or bounces.

After that, we've decided to hit the graveyard, even though we're missing Savage.

"His party must be in full swing now," I say.

"Who cares," Beaterson says.

All I wan-na do is beeeeat you,
All I wan-na do is complete you.

Deshutsis is doing this quietly, sort of under his breath. It's almost more irritating that way than when he sings at normal volume.

All I wan-na do is best ya
All I wan-na do is test ya.

Beaterson is staring straight ahead. The muscles in his jaw are working.

"Flint, ask him to stop."

"Dwight," I say. "Have some humility. Come on, we're asking you nicely."

Deshutsis snickers. "Some people can dish it out, but they sure can't take it."

All I wan-na do is muss ya
All I wan-na do is cuss ya.

All I wan-na do is cream you
All I wan-na do is dreeeeeeam you.

Suddenly, Beaterson swerves the car over to the side of the road and slams on the brakes. We go into a fishtailing screech, and he practically loses it on the shoulder, but he gets it under control. The car comes to a full stop.

"Not good for the brakes," Deshutsis says.

"Get out."

Deshutsis, sort of laughing, turns his head toward Beaterson.

"Relax," Deshutsis says. "Take a pink pill."

"I said get out of my car."

Deshutsis lets out some short exhalations of breath. A nervous laugh.

"Get out," Beaterson says again.

Deshutsis says, "All right, all right. Just drive. I'm sorry, I won't do it again. You win. I surrender."

"Get out."

"Forget you."

"I said get out, and I mean it, Deshutsis."

"No way."

"Get out of my car. I'm not kidding."

"Hey, come on, I said I'd stop doing it. You don't have to make a big scene. I hate scenes."

I'm starting to feel my forehead get clammy. I think Beaterson really has lost it.

"Let's just call a time-out here for a second," I say.

"Let's all take a deep breath," Deshutsis says.

"No, you're getting out. I'm sick of you. I swear to God, Deshutsis, I'm sick of everything you do. You annoy me in every way. I'm sick of asking you to do something and hearing you give me some kind of smart-ass come-back. I'm sick of your face, I'm sick of your voice, I'm sick of all your mannerisms and tics. I'm sick of how you lied to us about Goon, and about his cabin, and about his ability, and how you wasted our time. And—and here's the thing. I warned you. I told you if you didn't stop singing I would throw you out, and now I'm following through on that."

Deshutsis laughs. "Oh, I get it. You're trying to make some kind of point. This all has to do with what we should do about Savage, doesn't it? Tough love! Right? You're trying to prove some point about tough love. Like every action has a consequence. Brilliant! You had me. Okay, okay, you've made your point. You win. I will totally zip up my mouth."

"Listen," Beaterson says, and he's shaking all over. "I'm going to say this one more time. If you don't get the fuck out of my car, I'm going to come over there and drag you out, so help me God."

"I can't get out here. We're in the middle of no-where."

"Come on," I say. "Let's skip dropping the bowl-ing ball and just go to the graveyard. That'll calm us all down."

"I'm not going anywhere until he gets out."

"Why are you being so damn touchy?" Deshutsis says. "What's the problem? Do you want to talk about it?"

"Dwight, I think you're just making it worse," I say. "Why don't you go ahead and step out of the car and take a walk, while Rick and I have a talk."

"No way," Deshutsis says. "He'll drive off and leave me out here."

Beaterson says nothing. Instead, he grabs his cowboy hat, puts it on, gets out, and walks away.

Deshutsis and I just sit here.

"Let him cool off," Deshutsis says. "Why did he buy that cowboy hat, anyway? Don't you think it was kind of scary, him buying that hat? Well, I think I'll get out and stretch the old legbos, too. If I'm not back in twenty minutes, I've probably been abducted."

He gets out, shuts the door, and takes off, walking in the opposite direction from Beaterson. And I sit back and let out a long rush of air.

21

I don't know how long I've been sitting here. It's kind of a pleasant night, though, not cold at all. Very few cars have come by in either direction. It's pretty rural out here. In fact, we're not far from the ravine road where I towed Savage the other night.

I notice a car coming. Its headlights aren't on—just its yellow fog lights.

It looks like a luxury car. It drives by very slowly. A few minutes later, it comes back the other way, going just as slow. I can't see inside, but I can hear music pounding from it, and as it crawls by, I get an uneasy feeling.

Pretty soon I hear the *scrutch-scrutch* of footsteps coming from behind. It's Deshutsis.

He climbs into the front seat. He's breathing fairly heavily from walking, and his face is flushed.

"He's not back yet?"

"No."

"You know what?"

"What?"

"I think we spend an inordinate amount of time trying to figure each other out."

"I don't know about that," I say.

"Oh, yes, you better believe it. Of course, some of us are more high-maintenance than others. Like Beaterson and Savage. We're always having to put up with their little mood swings. You and I are solid. We're simple souls. Low-maintenance."

I laugh.

"What are you laughing at?"

"You, low-maintenance? You know how much effort and willpower it takes me on a regular basis to keep from strangling you?"

"Just because I beat you at bowling," he says.

"No, it's your whole . . . being."

"Oh. Gee, thanks."

"Like at the lake today," I say.

"What about the lake today?"

"It's a perfect example. Cream soda. You had to ask for cream soda."

"So?"

"You go over to some guy's dad's house. I mean, the dad just got divorced. The guy's trying to glue his life back together, and here you come and ask for cream soda, but if he doesn't have that, you'll settle for root beer, but only if it's A&W. I wanted to throw you in the lake."

"Are you finished?" he says.

"Yes."

Deshutsis is looking out the window. He's jiggling his leg up and down. Thinking about what he's going to say. His comeback. He's always got a comeback.

"It's not all one-sided," he finally says. "There are things about you that infuriate me, you know. You want some examples?"

"Not really," I say.

"For example: you always take Beaterson's side against me. Ever notice that? I think you're afraid if you contradict him, it'll set him off. Another example: the way you talk to people. You have this superior attitude. Like today at the lake, with Goon. You made me sick. You just made me want to puke."

I don't mention to Deshutsis that I agree with him; I had the same feeling about myself at the lake today.

"The way you talked to Goon," he says. "Polite, but superior. 'Hey, Tim? Buddy? Would you mind washing off the ball, buddy? So I don't have to touch your dirt and filth?' 'We can't use you, Tim.' 'Sorry, Tim. You're a real nice guy, but you're not good enough for us.' Like you think you're Mr. High Class. It just made my stomach crawl. I was ashamed. Of all the condescending, patronizing snobs. Like you're some kind of holy, pure, older brother. Our captain. Captain Flint. You know what you are? You're a royal prig. That's the word I'm looking for. *Prig.*"

I look down at my bowling ball. It's glowing in the dark, like a full moon, and the three holes are like craters, the man in the moon.

From out of the darkness, Beaterson is coming toward us along the road, wearing his cowboy hat.

He reaches the car, opens the door, and slides in. He takes off his cowboy hat. He sits for a moment looking straight ahead. The silence is thick.

"What's up," he says.

"Just having a little gut-letting here," Deshutsis says. "We should have a Yanni tape playing in the background."

"I'm all right now," Beaterson says. His voice is calm and quiet. "I think that little overpass is just a mile or two up the road."

"Let's go, then," I say.

Beaterson doesn't move. He sighs. "You know what today was? Saturday morning. My favorite time of the week, my favorite time of the year. College football. I was watching a college game. Real football. Real contact. Hitting and tackling."

I think I know where this is going.

Beaterson continues. "Cheerleaders, fans. The band. Thousands of students. Cheering for the gods. Doesn't that ever get to you? Here we are playing flag football. Do you ever feel like you made a huge mistake in going with flag football over real football?"

"Like about every day," I say.

Beaterson turns around and looks at me. "No."

"Every day," I repeat.

"You regret it, then? You feel like you made the wrong choice?"

"I could have played high-school football, that's for sure," I say. "We both could have."

"Why didn't we, then?" he says.

"Because we didn't," I say. "I followed Glen Como, and I guess you followed me. I don't know whether it was a mistake or not. What I mean is, every day, the thought crosses my mind, and I wonder about it. I'm not saying I like real football better than flag. I love flag football. Maybe having all those cheering fans and the glory, that would be great. Yeah, I regret not having that. But I don't know if it would be better. Maybe the physical hitting and the discipline of being on the school team, maybe that would be better for me. But I don't know if it would be better than the feeling I get when I play flag football. I could have lettered, but so what? When I play flag, I play every down, I call the plays, I'm happy. But that's me. You have to decide for yourself. You could turn out for football. It might be too late this season, I don't know, but you could do it next year when we're seniors. You'd be a starting linebacker, we all know that. If you told Coach Millner you wanted to play on his team, he'd have an orgasm."

"Do you think if I did that, and I had a good year, I could get a scholarship somewhere, you know, Wyoming or Montana?"

"Maybe," I say. "You've already got the cowboy hat; you'd fit right in."

Deshutsis clears his throat. "I—"

"Don't make a speech," Beaterson says.

"I won't. But let me at least say something."

"Just watch yourself," Beaterson says.

"Yeah, yeah. We go back a long way. All the way to first grade. Can you believe that? But you know what? Next year we're seniors, and then that's it, we're gone. You realize that? You'll go to some redneck college, whether you get a scholarship or not, because that's what you want. Me, I'm going somewhere just the opposite—some inner-city urban college. I want diversity. Racial, cultural—there's solid evidence that having racial and cultural diversity gives you a better education. And Flint, I don't know what you'll do, but you'll go your own way. I mean, for a long time I've been thinking we have this problem—we're too much the same, we're not exposed to diversity, we're not open to new experiences. But this is it. We've got this season, and we've got next season, and then it's over. Talk about radical change. And I think Flint's right. We can think about how things might have turned out different, but the bottom line is, things are the way they are. This is who we are. Why? Who the hell knows? Because that's how it worked out, that's why. Instead of griping about how narrow and limited we are, I ought to be marveling at how amazing it is that three people as weird and different as we are could possibly manage to stay friends since first grade. I know I said I wasn't going to make a speech, but who was I kidding, we all knew I would."

"Is that the end of it?" Beaterson says.

"Yeah, how was I? Was it as good for you as it was for me?"

"You want a letter grade or a score?" Beaterson says.

"A hug would be nice."

Beaterson throws his head back and laughs for a long time. When he's finished, he reaches for the key and starts the car, glances in his side mirror, and pulls out into the road. That same car is coming toward us slowly, no headlights.

"What the hell is this?" Beaterson says. "I noticed this car when I was walking."

"So did I," Deshutsis says.

"Somebody being cute," Beaterson says. He flashes his headlights at it several times as the car passes. Suddenly, it whips around and its horn is blaring from behind us. Its brights come on, lighting up the whole interior of Beaterson's car.

"Jesus!" Beaterson jumps. He pulls over to the shoulder to let the car pass, but it pulls over right behind him, almost touching his rear bumper. Its high beams are blinding. The driver lays on his horn.

"What the—" Beaterson says.

"Gang initiation rite," Deshutsis says in a tense, hushed voice.

Squinting into his side mirror, Beaterson eases back onto the road and speeds up, but the car follows us, those brights flooding in. Beaterson goes faster; the car stays right on us. I feel myself instinctively ducking, like any second there're going to be bullets coming through the rear window.

Beaterson, muttering to himself, lets up on the gas pedal and slows back down to a crawl.

"What are you doing?" Deshutsis says. "Keep going. Speed up. What are you doing?"

The car pulls alongside us on our left. It looks like a BMW. The front and rear windows go down, revealing four guys, more or less our age, giving us the evil eye. Two are wearing baseball caps backward.

Beaterson comes to a complete stop; so do they. We're side-by-side in the middle of the road.

A smart-ass voice says, "Who taught you to drive that heap, your grandma?"

Beaterson says, "Your mom's pimp let you borrow the car tonight?"

"Eat me."

"You want to step out and settle it?" Beaterson says.

"Sounds good to me. Pull over."

"You got it." Beaterson eases his car over onto the shoulder.

"Don't do this," Deshutsis says in a quavery voice.

"Shut up."

Instead of pulling over, though, the BMW drives up alongside us, and one of the guys in the backseat pops his head and shoulders up through the sun roof and lets fly a bottle. The bottle hits the hood of Beaterson's car and shatters, throwing beer suds and glass against the windshield. We all jump. The BMW peels out, its taillights receding in the darkness ahead.

Beaterson starts muttering again in that clenched, trembling voice, and I know we're in trouble.

Suddenly, he floors it, and the chase is on.

22

"Is this worth it?" Deshutsis says.

"Let it go," I hear myself saying, trying to keep my voice calm and even. "Not worth the gas."

Beaterson is leaning forward, clutching the wheel, and driving too fast. We're on the same winding ravine road that I came down a couple of nights ago in my dad's Explorer.

"Don't be an ass, slow down," Deshutsis says. "You're going to get us killed."

"People carry guns nowadays," I say.

"That's right," Deshutsis says. "Even little dickbrains like them."

"Shut up," Beaterson says. "Both of you. I get tired of you both whimpering all the time. Neither one of you has a pair of balls between you."

"Spare us the balls talk," I say, holding on to my bowling ball to keep it from rolling around.

If this were a highway, the BMW would eat it up

and be long gone. But on this winding road, its brake lights keep flaring, and there aren't any side roads.

The road is straight when it gets to the bottom of the ravine, and we should be able to see the BMW's taillights, but there's no sign of it.

Beaterson slows down. "Those idiots," he says. "They've turned down there."

He's right. Instead of following the road straight up out of the ravine, they've taken a right, down the dead end. The same one I came down the other night to get Savage.

"I don't like this," I say.

"This smells like a trap," Deshutsis says.

"A trap," Beaterson says. "They don't know where the hell they are. They're probably from Bellevue or Mercer Island."

Again, he's probably right about their not knowing it's a dead end. I remember that the sign had been knocked over.

Beaterson turns off his headlights and just stays put in the road.

"What are you doing?" Deshutsis says.

"Let's bag this," I say.

"Yeah, they're from the east side somewhere," Beaterson mutters. "Microsoft brats. Redmond or Mercer Island or Issaquah. Pricks."

"They're not worth this," I say, but he's not listening.

Maybe he's remembering the time we went to a play in Issaquah that his sister had a big part in, and during the intermission, we overheard two women talking and laughing in the lobby. One was saying how Sari Beaterson was a pretty good actress but too bad she was so homely; the other was saying, "Homely? My God, that's not the word for it!"

With his lights off, Beaterson turns the wheel and starts creeping down the road in total darkness. After half a mile or so, we can see the taillights of the BMW. It's stopped in that little turnaround where Savage had parked two nights ago with Kat Olney before he rolled into the creek bed. They've obviously figured out that they can't go any farther, but I can't tell whether they're trying to turn around or they're just waiting until it's good and safe to go back on the main road. There's no way they can see Beaterson's car creeping up in the dark. They're either very drunk or very lost. Or armed.

"I'm not with you on this," I say. "This is just stupid."

"I agree," Deshutsis says. "This sucks. Your sister would agree."

"My sister," Beaterson spits. "Don't convoke the name of my sister.

"I believe you mean *in*voke, not *con*voke," Deshutsis says.

"You're both pussies."

"That's a meaningless label," I say.

"No, it isn't," Beaterson says. "Either you've got pride or you don't. You don't have to help me. You can just stay in the car. I won't have any respect for you, but that's all right."

When he's just a few feet from the BMW, Beaterson turns on his headlights. The BMW is pinned. They can't go forward, and they can't back up.

Beaterson puts on his cowboy hat and gets out.

Deshutsis and I just sit here.

Deshutsis starts swearing. He looks at me. His face is pure white. Finally, he gets out.

So, I have no other choice. I get out, too.

The three of us approach the BMW. The four guys are just sitting in there with the windows rolled up. The motor is running. They haven't made any attempt to get out.

Beaterson knocks on the driver's window. I'm waiting for the gunshot.

"Excuse me."

"Let us alone!" somebody yells from inside the BMW. "I have a phone. I'll call the police."

"You change your mind about stepping out of your car?" Beaterson says.

"Yes. We didn't mean it. We were just joking. My

friend didn't mean to throw that bottle. He's drunk. He doesn't know what he's doing. Hey, look, man, I apologize. Let's just be cool about this."

Beaterson stands there with his hands on his hips, shaking his head. "Are you all gutless?" he says.

They don't say anything.

"Where's your pride?" Beaterson says.

"Hey, man, I didn't mean to hit your car, I swear. I wasn't aiming for your car."

Beaterson turns to me and Deshutsis. "Should we accept their apology and forget about the whole thing? Or should we make them suffer the consequences of their actions?"

"They're suffering now," I say. "Let's get out of here."

Beaterson turns around and heads back to his car. Deshutsis and I follow.

When Beaterson gets to his car, he opens the rear door, reaches inside, and picks something up. It's my bowling ball.

"Hey," I say cautiously.

"Don't worry, I'll bring it right back."

"Hey," I say again. "Come on. Not Proud Jerry."

"Let's give Proud Jerry something to be proud about," Beaterson says.

He carries the ball over to the BMW. He raises it above his head, and brings it down full force on the trunk of the BMW. There's a *bang*. Then he slams it against the

182

rear window. *Crack.* The window crinkles, but doesn't shatter. There is silence from inside the BMW.

Beaterson is now holding half of a bowling ball. The ball has busted in half. The inside of it is black. The other half of the ball is somewhere on the ground, but I can't see it.

Beaterson carries the chunk of ball to us and drops it into the backseat.

"I guess that proves that bowling balls don't bounce," he says.

He gets in behind the wheel and we drive off.

He doesn't say anything until we're back on the main road.

"Three bad gringos, that's what we are," he says. "I knew you guys wouldn't pussy-out on me. I knew you'd get out with me. You didn't want to do it, but you stood with me, watching my back. We three bad gringos," he says. "Three bad clams, that's us. Hey! You know what we got? You know what we got?"

"Half a bowling ball," I say.

"We got balls!" he yells. "We might have half a bowling ball, but we got us a big old pair of Proud Jerrys."

"So what?" Deshutsis says.

"So what? I'll tell you so what. Dwight, you can actually go home tonight, and you can look at yourself in the mirror, and you can say, 'I got balls!' That's so what. The next time you bake cookies for a girl, you don't have to worry about your manhood. And you know what else? We just proved that we have something Rachel Summerfield doesn't have. What are we afraid of? Why should we be intimidated by Rachel Summerfield? You know what I think we should do? I think we should be men. Sign her. Dump Savage, go with Summerfield. *I'll* hike the ball. I'm the one who should do it, a wide-body like me, I'll plug up the middle, let Rachel and Dwight run the patterns and get open. She wants to play quarterback sometimes? Let her. When you have pride in yourself, you can make sacrifices. Are we men enough to let Summerfield become one of us? Are we?"

"Yes," Deshutsis says. "Yes."

"You better believe it. Flint? . . . Hey, Flint."

"What?"

Beaterson's looking at me. "What do you say? Should we go find a pay phone?"

I shake my head. I've had it. "Not until I talk to Savage first."

"What for?" Beaterson says.

"I don't know. I just want to talk to him."

"All right, then," Beaterson says. "Talk to him first, if that's how you want to do it. But don't let Summerfield get away."

I nod. "Let's go to the graveyard."

Later, Beaterson pulls over onto the gravel shoulder next to the cemetery and cuts the engine. We crawl through an opening in the bushes, Beaterson leading the way with a tiny flashlight. When we emerge from the bushes, the whole hillside of graves is lit up by the moon, and fog is rising from the ground. It's very spooky. We walk among the graves until we find Glen Como's.

Beaterson points the flashlight at it to make sure. It's just a small slab, with Glen's name and dates. Beaterson turns off the flashlight. We stand in a straight line, facing the headstone. We unzip, aim, and start peeing. I look up at the moon, and out at the layer of fog on the ground. Our splashing sounds seem to make a tremendous noise in this silence.

It's not a contest or a race. Actually, I'm not sure what it is anymore, or what it ever was. It just seems like an empty ritual, one of those ceremonies you do out of tradition but you can't really say why. In a few years, we'll remember this cemetery, but we'll hardly remember this night or this weekend. These thoughts are strong in me right now, very strange and mysterious.

Do we really know each other now? I think so. I think we know each other about as well as anybody can know someone. We've spent our whole lives together. In a way, we're closer even than brothers.

"Well," Beaterson says, breaking the silence. Even the zipping sound of his fly seems loud. "There's one thing I can't exactly see Summerfield doing with us."

23

Sunday morning, driving into Savage's neighborhood, I pass the doughnut shop where Thor Hupf works. I can't resist. A doughnut sounds good right now.

I park and go inside, and there's Thor, sitting on a stool with a book propped open on his lap. He's snoozing. The title of the book is *Thermonuclear Reactors*.

No one else is in the place.

Thor's eyes flutter open and focus on me.

"Hey, Flint."

"Thor."

"You haven't come here to wreak vengeance on me or something, have you?" he says.

"No."

"Oh, good. You going to give me another chance to try out for your team?"

"No."

"Well, what brings you here, then?"

"Doughnuts."

"Oh. Yeah."

I scan the usual selection inside the glass case. "Cade have his party last night?" I ask.

Thor shakes his head slowly. "Oh. Oh ho ho."

"What?" I say. "Somebody die?"

"Oh. Flint."

"I'll take two of those and two of those," I say. "And two of those."

Thor snatches the doughnuts with tongs and bags them.

"You want some coffee or something?" he says.

"No, how about a large milk."

He puts a carton of 2 percent in the sack.

"So, what happened?" I say.

He leans toward me.

"It was the best of parties, and it was the worst of parties. I mean, everybody was there at some point. Everybody. Guys I haven't seen for years. Guys I've never seen but heard about. Big shots. Pedro Hawkins, remember him? And the Iguana brothers. And Chivera."

"Chivera?"

"Chivera. Can you believe it? But wait. Remember that PE teacher we had in middle school who got busted for smoking pot in the locker room?"

"Mr. Devlin?"

"Mr. Devlin was there."

"No."

"Yeah! Mr. Devlin. He was there with this Swiss supermodel. And Deshutsis's brother was there, Bob. With that girlfriend of his."

"Missy."

"Yeah, Missy. I even saw some people from the Junior Science Symposium. There were three or four kegs. Girls everywhere. Girls dancing. Full moon. Girls, packed in like sardines! But then it started to deteriorate. Things got out of control. They started moshing in the living room. Some losers started a food fight in the kitchen—they got into the cereal, the flour, the eggs, the honey. I'm surprised the house is still standing. I don't know what happened to Cade, but the last time I saw him, he was passed out and being carried to his bedroom. That is one party I will tell my grandchildren about."

When I ask Thor how much for the milk and doughnuts, he waves his hand and says forget it. "I owe you for Friday night," he says. "That was low, what I did to you."

"Thanks, Thor."

"No problem. Doughnuts are good for you. That's why I work here. I like to help my fellow man."

"Hey, Thor?"

"Yeah?"

"You know those girls who were in your van?"

"Yeah?"

"The one named Malibu?"

"Yeah?"

"I'd never met her before, but I'm glad I did. There was something I liked about her."

"I know what you mean."

"I just wanted to tell somebody that, so I'm telling you."

He nods. "Okay."

"It would have been good having you on our flag-football team," I say.

"I know it."

"It's just that we have a uh . . ."

"Low tolerance for drunkenness and drug use?" he says.

"Yeah, that's it."

"Hey, Flint?"

"Yeah?"

"You're not by any chance on your way to Cade's house, are you?"

"Yes, I am."

"You still planning to kick him off your team?"

"I don't know yet. It looks like it."

"Well, it's none of my business, but I think that little sucker really looks up to you. Big time."

I eat the first doughnut and wash it down with ice-cold milk as I cruise through Cade's neighborhood, past the depressing bingo hall that used to be a bag-it-yourself grocery store, past the shabby old Viva Theater that's been beaten down from years of showing nothing but kiddie flicks.

Parked on the street in front of Cade's house is the idiotic boat and trailer that Cade's dad bought with his inheritance money. It's one of those long, black, sparkly drag boats. The name stenciled on the back is *Savage Sucka.*

Cade's lime-green Camaro is sitting in the driveway. He's got a bumper sticker on it that says UNLESS YOU'RE A HEMORRHOID, GET OFF MY ASS.

The front yard is littered with cups, cans, and bottles. A car ashtray has been emptied on the driveway.

I knock on the door and wait. I have to rap several times before Cade finally shows up. He's holding a can of beer. His eyes look swollen and unfocused. He's wearing fluorescent orange shorts cut below his knees, no shirt. He's got the torso of a teeny Mr. America, and he still has his waterskier's suntan. He's wearing a string of puka shells around his neck.

"You missed a kick-ass party." That's all he says. Then he takes a swig from the can. "Guess who was here last night?"

"Who?"

"Blake Butterworth."

"Wow."

190

"Jocks, cheerleaders, big shots." He names off a who's-who list similar to Thor's. His big finale is Bob Deshutsis and Missy; then, for his encore, Mr. Devlin.

"You shoulda seen Devlin's woman. She's a Swedish porno star."

We go into the house. The living room looks like it's been trashed, ransacked, and turned upside down by the CIA searching for microfilm. It smells like stale beer that's been poured into a tennis shoe that had previously been used as an ashtray.

"You've got a mess here."

"Understatement of the day," he says.

"Doughnut?"

I hold the bag open. He helps himself and takes a bite, and chases it with a drink of beer. My stomach wishes it hadn't seen that.

"We need to talk," I say.

"Yeah, I know."

"I really don't want to sound like your old lady," I say.

He nods. "I didn't plan it," he says. "It all just happened. It fell into my lap. It's not every day somebody like Bao Alatina says he'll help me throw the party to end all parties. It was all worth it. Blake Butterworth was here. In my bathroom. Sitting on the edge of my bathtub, smoking a doobie, with me. *Me.* And Chivera. Me and Chivera stood in my backyard, the two of us, side-by-side, like old friends or something, taking a leak and looking at the moon."

"All that, and then you passed out."

His face darkens. "I thought you weren't going to sound like my old lady."

"I lied."

"Don't make fun of me. Beaterson and Deshutsis, that's all they do. They never let up on me. I get tired of it. Every little thing I do, they make fun of it."

"We could have talked about all this," I say.

"We are."

"You could have told me about the party when we were at The Coffee Spot. Why didn't you tell me?"

"It wasn't a done deal at that point. Besides, if I'd said anything, you would have tried to talk me out of it. You would've made threats. You would have given me an ultimatum. 'You don't do what I say, I'll kick your ass off the team, and I'll tell Beaterson and Deshutsis about Kat Olney.' Blah blah blah. I didn't want all that distraction and hassle."

"You don't care about anybody but yourself, do you?" I say.

He laughs. "I bet you three have been clucking like a bunch of old hens all weekend," he says. "Three old biddies on the prayer chain. What to do about old Cade."

"It hurts," I say.

"What hurts?"

"Having you just turn your back and walk out on us."

"Yeah, I bet it's real painful."

"You're a mess," I say.

"Thanks, Ma."

"How could you let them trash your place? Your own *house*? You think Blake Butterworth gives a rip about you? Chivera? Bob Deshutsis? You think Alatina cares about you? Who are your friends? Them or us?"

He looks off to the side.

"Them or us?" I say. "Come on. Who cares about you?"

"Nobody."

"We do, you stupid idiot. It's us."

Cade eases himself onto the edge of the coffee table, and rubs his face. When he looks up, his face is drained and his eyes are really bloodshot.

His voice sounds hollow. "You guys don't care about me. I'm the Oyster. That's all I am. The extra body. You put up with me, because you have to. If you could get rid of me for somebody better, you'd do it. Friday night, you guys didn't waste any time. It took you about three seconds to get on the phone to Thor. Don't tell me you care about me. You've been wanting an excuse to dump me, and now you have it."

His face is ashen. His eyes go glassy. The life seems

to be slowly seeping out of him. He sways, still sitting there on the coffee table. He opens and closes his mouth, gulping. He bends over and looks at his shoes. I finally realize what's happening and lunge for a wastebasket, grab it, and drop it next to his feet just as he starts puking. Good-bye doughnut, good-bye beer.

I go and have a look at the kitchen. It's bad. The floor is layered with food, drawers have been opened and dumped out. Silverware. Everything. Total vandalism.

I want to get out of here.

Now he's moaning in the living room.

I really want to get out of here.

"Ohhhhhhhh. Ohhhhhhh."

The puke smell is drifting into the kitchen. Through the back door window I see sunlight in the backyard. I can escape.

I can call Summerfield—if it's not too late. If she hasn't given up on us. I can tell her I'll be at her house in ten minutes with all the forms she needs to fill out.

Back in the living room, I notice the cordless phone on the floor. Maybe it's busted. Yeah. It'll need recharging or something.

I see my bag of doughnuts on the coffee table, within splashing distance of the wastebasket. Cade is hunched over, trembling fiercely. This is horrible. I've got to get out of here. I want to tell him that he's a waste of a life. I miss Glen. We all do. Nobody would miss Cade. It would be a relief to be rid of him.

I go over and pick up the phone and press the talk button, hoping there won't be a dial tone. But it works. So I start punching a number.

24

"**What're you** doing?" I ask Beaterson when he answers the phone.

"Sitting here in my shorts. You know what I'm looking at?"

"Your shorts?"

"No. Pancakes. Just like the picture on the box. That's what I told my sister this morning. Make me a stack just like that picture on that damn box. And she did it. Butter and syrup and everything. And there's a game on the tube I'm waiting for. What's up?"

"I'm here at Savage's. He's, uh . . ."

"Down on his scabby little knees begging and sobbing for just one more chance and you're wavering. You are slush."

"Well, not exactly."

"Not exactly what?"

"He's in pretty bad shape. They trashed his house last night."

"So?"

"He's going to need some serious help getting this place cleaned up."

I hear Beaterson let out a long sigh. I know exactly what he's thinking, because I'm thinking it, too. This is Savage's mess. His choice.

"I take it you haven't dumped him yet," Beaterson says.

"It's hard to talk to somebody when he's got his head stuck in a wastebasket."

"He's got his head stuck somewhere, all right," Beaterson says. "Do you know how pretty this stack of pancakes is?"

"As pretty as on the box," I say.

Another sigh. "Okay. Give me a little bit."

"Enjoy those pancakes," I say. "And bring cleaning supplies."

"Are you still in bed?"

There's silence on the other end of the phone, which makes me think Deshutsis has fallen back to sleep.

"You there?" I say.

"Yes, I am still in bed. It's called sleeping in. Great solitary pastime. All it takes is a bed and a rare occurrence called Sunday morning."

"I'm at Savage's."

"Good for you."

"He's a mess. He's sick. He's got a major problem."

"Tell me something I don't know. But don't tell me till around noon."

"His house got trashed; it's a disaster. His folks are getting back from Reno tomorrow afternoon."

"Tell him to call Alatina."

"I called Beaterson. He's—"

"No."

"—on his way over with some—"

"No, no, no."

"—cleaning supplies."

"Negative. You're breaking up, bravo-one-niner, you're breaking up. *Kchgrrrrkchgrrrrrchkrrrrrrr.*"

Deshutsis is doing a pretty good imitation of static.

I wait for him to stop.

"It's trashed," I say.

"My heart goes out to him."

I carry the phone into the kitchen. With every drawer and cupboard open, it's easy to look for cleaning supplies. My shoes crunch on the floor with each footstep, and sticky stuff is accumulating on my soles. I throw open the back door to let in some air.

Cade staggers in from the living room, holding his stomach and shivering. His face is drained, and his eyes are puffy slits.

I'm still holding the phone to my ear, even though Deshutsis hung up a minute ago.

In between dry heaves, Cade has managed to help me find the buckets, rags, mop, broom, various cleaning chemicals, and a useless vacuum cleaner held together by duct tape. I remember to call and cancel the two remaining practice games we had scheduled for today.

As I open the drapes on the front window, I see Deshutsis tramping up the walkway. In one hand he's got a plastic garbage bag filled with stuff. In the other he's carrying a black upright vacuum cleaner that is so space-age and futuristic it's scary.

He shoves the door open with his foot

"Where's Beaterson?"

"You beat him here."

"Where's the midget?"

"I told him to go lie down and see if he can grow a new stomach."

Deshutsis surveys the house with an expression so beyond disgust, it ages his face by about forty years. From the sack he pulls out a six-pack of bottled cream soda and a stack of CDs. He goes over to the stereo and inserts several of the CDs from his stack.

He reaches back into his plastic sack. This time he comes out with a pair of elbow-length yellow rubber gloves, which he slowly and carefully pulls onto each hand like a giant condom.

He looks at me. "What? These are Rubbermaids. Best you can get."

A few minutes later, Beaterson walks in, wearing his cowboy hat. He stands in the doorway and tips his hat back and whistles.

"Looks like a fine time was had by all." His eyes land on Deshutsis. "Nice pair of Maidenforms. You got a frilly little apron to go with those?"

"They're Rubbermaids."

"So flexible you can pick your nose with them," Beaterson says.

Deshutsis has found the stereo remote control, and he points it at the stereo, but hesitates. "When all is said and done, he won't even thank us for this."

"Yes, he will," I say.

"You wanna bet?"

"Gentlemen's bet," I say, which means we bet nothing but our honor.

"Five bucks," Deshutsis says.

"All right," I say. "Five bucks."

Deshutsis comes over to me and peels off the right glove. It makes a *shlup*. We shake on the bet. He tugs the glove back on, then aims the remote at the stereo. But the phone starts ringing. Beaterson finds it on the windowsill.

"Savage residence," he says, and listens for a while. "Sure. You bet. All right."

He puts the phone down and looks at us.

"If we find a chartreuse sweater with reindeers on the shoulders, it belongs to somebody named Heather. What's chartreuse, anyway? Is that like magenta?"

"It's bright greenish yellow," Deshutsis says.

"Yeah, that's magenta," Beaterson says.

"Magenta is purplish red," says Deshutsis.

"No, it isn't. Magenta is a yellowy green," Beaterson says. "Like mauve. That's one I know for a fact."

"You're loco," Deshutsis says. "It's a combination of purple and red."

"Bet?"

"I'll bet you fifty bucks."

"All right," Beaterson says. "Shake on it."

Deshutsis strides across the room to Beaterson and sticks out his hand. Beaterson pulls back. "Take that thing off."

Deshutsis sighs. Holding up his hand, he *shlups* off the glove finger by finger. He extends his bare hand. "Fifty big ones," he says. "Flint is a witness to this."

I'm a witness, all right. I saw it coming a mile away. The amazing thing is that Deshutsis didn't.

Beaterson slowly moves his head back and forth, raises his hands, and says in a lispy voice, "I just wanted to see you take it off again. It's such a turn-on."

Deshutsis mutters while he puts the glove back on.

The vacuum cleaner Deshutsis brought has dual upright clear tubes, half-filled with water and filtered air; a three-speed supercharged motor; a self-propelling drive line; two headlamps; black wheel covers; and a sloped motor housing that looks like the front end of a '66 Corvette Stingray. The brand name on it says WHISPER QUIET. Deshutsis turns it on, and, true to its name, it starts whispering.

Beaterson and I can only marvel at it.

"That is one nice vacuum cleaner," Beaterson says.

"Whisper quiet," Deshutsis says.

"What?" Beaterson says.

"Whisper quiet."

"Hah?"

"I said, *whisper quiet!*"

"Turn that damn thing off, I can't hear you!"

I'm filling garbage sacks and piling them up in the drive-way, where we'll have to transfer them to our car trunks and take them to the dump.

Last time I checked on Cade, he was sprawled face-down on his bed, sound asleep. I noticed his oil painting of the original Charlie's Angels that he bought at the

Goodwill for ten dollars a few months ago. Someone has taken the lit end of a cigarette and burned a hole in each one of the Angels' pupils. Now they stare as if possessed. I doubt his parents will notice. Actually, it's kind of an improvement.

Cade drags himself into the living room, carrying a bucket, and starts wiping the beer off the walls.

"Ohhhhhh. Ohhhhhhhh."

Deshutsis gives him a long look.

"Ohhhhhhhhh."

"Turn up the stereo," Deshutsis barks. "Where's the remote?"

"Ohhhhhhhh."

"Oh, go back to bed!" Deshutsis yells.

"Hey, look at me!" Beaterson says. He has stuffed two rags inside his shirt to look like boobs, and he's dancing with Deshutsis's vacuum cleaner. "I'm Tim Goon!"

Real time goes second by second, one second at a time, one beer cup, butt, bottle cap, candy wrapper, cereal flake, and potato chip at a time. There's no skipping, fast-forwarding, or cutting. No montage. Real time is reality. Reality can really bite.

It can smell bad, too.

I don't think this is what we had in mind when we said we were going to face reality this weekend.

Out in the backyard, I'm picking up litter and getting some fresh air. I notice a light green sweater hanging from the highest branch of a tree that has beautiful red and gold leaves that are falling. I climb the tree, just for the heck of it. Just for the Heather of it. Not bad. I smile at my own joke.

I can hear Beaterson and Deshutsis inside the house. They're arguing about something over the music. Or maybe it's music they're arguing over.

I like it up here in the tree, looking down on the yard. I would like to stay up here.

I'm just able to reach up and pluck the sweater off the branch with my first two fingers.

25

We're sitting around drinking bottles of cream soda. It's two in the afternoon. This house is so spotless that when Cade's parents walk in they will either die of shock or call the police, but that's not our problem.

Cade seems to be feeling a lot better. It's a miracle.

A few minutes ago I heard him talking on his cell phone to Heather, telling her he had found her sweater and he'd be glad to run it over to her. He hasn't left yet; right now, he's contemplating a cigarette burn in one of the couch cushions.

"I can't remember if my dad did that or if it happened last night."

"You just better hope they hit a few jackpots down there," Beaterson says.

Cade smiles sheepishly. "I, uh . . . I guess if you guys want to dump me, you might as well get it over with."

I look at Beaterson and Deshutsis. They don't say anything.

"Go ahead," Cade says. "I deserve it. I'm worthless. I know that. I can't explain the things I do. There's no explanation—I mean, I know what I do isn't rational."

"Do you want us to dump you?" Beaterson says.

Cade lowers his head. "It might be better that way."

"That's not what he asked," Deshutsis says. "Do you want off the team?"

"If I could trade, I would," he says. "I'd trade with Glen. I mean, I—"

"What's Glen got to do with anything?" Beaterson says.

"Let him finish," Deshutsis says, leaning forward. "Go ahead."

"I think about him every day," Cade says. His eyes are welling up. "He haunts me. I see him—just before I go off to sleep. I see his eye. That one eye. Nothing but white, no eyeball. I hear the sound of his head hitting. Sometimes . . . I don't know. It makes me do crazy things. I need your guys's help."

"How?" Beaterson says.

Cade shakes his head. "I don't know. Start by telling me the truth. Tell me you know how worthless I am, and that you're pissed at me because I killed Glen."

"You didn't kill Glen," Deshutsis says. "Nobody thinks you killed Glen."

"If I could trade places with him . . ."

"Yeah, you said that," Deshutsis says.

Cade buries his face in his hands. "I need help."

"You're beyond help," Beaterson says.

"I want to stay off the booze. I don't know if I can or not. I'm nothing. I'm just so—"

"Knock it off," Deshutsis says. "Stop talking like that."

"You're not that worthless," Beaterson says.

"I can't face it by myself anymore."

"We can help you," Beaterson says.

"That's what we're here for," Deshutsis says.

"Look," Beaterson says, "go and drop off that sweater to old Heather. While you're gone, we'll talk it over."

Cade shakes his head. "I've wasted your whole weekend—"

"Shut up," Beaterson says.

"It hasn't been a total waste," Deshutsis says. "Or maybe we needed to lose a weekend. Maybe we needed to have everything come to a screeching halt, so we could take a step back, take some inventory. Do a reality check."

"I know we've learned one thing," Beaterson says. "We learned that somebody as classy and talented as Rachel Summerfield wants to be on our team. And I'm not afraid to have her, either. But now I think we're stuck with each other. That's all right with me. Not because we feel sorry for you or think you need our help or whatever. We're stuck with you because we want you."

Cade wipes his face. "I won't let you guys down again."

"You do, you'll regret it," Beaterson says.

Deshutsis leans back in his chair and crosses his legs. He's got a trace of a smile.

"How about I bring back a pizza," Cade says. "Then later we could get some practice in under the lights. Go over our plays and everything."

There's a long stretch of silence, and it takes me a while before I realize that everyone's staring at me, as if they're waiting for me to say something. Cade is leaning forward, looking at me intently.

I feel a laugh coming from my belly. A big, gushing rumble, working its way up through my throat to my mouth, and I open up my mouth, tip my head back, and out it comes. Laughter. I'm laughing so hard I'm crying. I'm laughing so hard, I almost choke on the phlegm. As I laugh, I'm aware of everyone staring at me in disbelief.

"Oh," I say. "Oh. Oh, that was beautiful. That was so touching. That was a Hallmark moment. That had to be, without a doubt, the biggest pile of crap I have ever heard in my life."

"What?" Cade says.

"You're history," I say.

Cade laughs, hesitantly. "Huh?" he says. He looks at Beaterson and Deshutsis, who are both studying me.

"Cade," I say, "you are classic. You are schmaltzier

than a TV evangelist. You're a one-man Vegas nightclub act. I can't believe anybody could fall for your crap, let alone Beaterson and Deshutsis."

"It's the truth!" Cade yells. "Everything I said was true!"

"I'm not saying it isn't true. I'm just saying it's crap, and you pile it on as fast as you can shovel it. You use it to get what you want. It's so obvious, the way you just *manipulated* these two saps, and the amazing thing is that these two just sat there and let you make saps out of them. You trashed them, just like you let your own house get trashed. The only thing you said that was an outright lie was that you'd never let us down again. Of course you will. You'll do it whenever you feel like it. Something'll come along and fall in your lap, and we'll yell at you, and you'll tell us how worthless and haunted you are, and how you hear that *sound*, and we'll forgive you. You don't have a morsel of pride, and that lets you get away with anything you want. You can trash your own life, but you're not going to trash mine. I've still got my pride."

Cade's face is stricken. It hurts me to look at it. It hurts a lot. But it also makes me see and think more clearly.

"You're a lowlife," I say, "and that's all you are, no matter how good your excuse is. And it's a great excuse— you're haunted by a kid who died, and that makes you free to be a lowlife. But we deserve better than you. Anybody. Tim Goon, Summerfield, Thor, anybody but you. In fact, I'd rather not play than have you on my team. I'd rather sit out. Hell, I'd even play soccer."

Cade's chest is heaving. "Don't do this to me. Please. I—I don't know what I'll do if you dump me."

"You'll think of something. I'm outa here. I'm going to call Summerfield. Not from here. I'll go find a pay phone. If she's still speaking to me, and if she still wants to be on our team, then I'm going to drive over to her house and sign her up. If she's changed her mind, I'll call Goon."

I take out my wallet and find a five-dollar bill, which I hand to Deshutsis.

"Here you go," I say. "You were right again."

Deshutsis looks at the five, then at me for a moment, then pockets it.

"Right about what?" Cade says.

I walk across the living room to the front door and open it. As I go out, before I close it behind me, the last thing I hear is Cade saying to Deshutsis, "What were you right about?"

26

The four of us are in Summerfield's yellow Nissan, heading for Astoria, Oregon, for our first tournament of the season. I'm in the front seat, and Beaterson and Deshutsis are in the back. Summerfield's driving habits are tough getting used to. She changes lanes a lot for no reason. She listens to smooth jazz, screeching saxophones, when it's her turn to put in a tape. She has a tendency to run stop signs. She doesn't like to eat while she drives, so whenever we stop for cheeseburgers, we have to sit in her car in the parking lot until she finishes her meal.

Which is what we're doing right now, somewhere halfway between Seattle and Astoria.

"I've got a good idea for a small business," she says. "A road-kill removal service. They go around and look for dead animals on the road and dispose of them, so drivers don't have to see them. Do you know what I'd call it?"

"Carcass Be Gone?" Deshutsis says.

"No," Summerfield says. "Search 'n Scrape."

"I like Carcass Be Gone better," Deshutsis says.

"I don't like either one," Beaterson says.

About a month ago, I went to Bob the barber and got a haircut. The next day, we played our first game of the season, against the Chimps, and we beat them, 41–14. I threw five touchdown passes—three to Summerfield, one to Deshutsis, and one to Beaterson. Summerfield also threw one to me. Beaterson did most, but not all, of the hiking.

Since that game, we've played three more, and won all three. We're off to a 4–0 start in regular season, tied for first with Marty's Texaco, who we're playing in two weeks.

Cade Savage has shown up at our two most recent games. He paced up and down the sideline shouting things at us, as if he were our coach. The last game, he brought a whopping seven doughnuts, each one a different flavor. Half of them had a bite taken out of them. Later, after Cade had left and it was just the four of us, Summerfield told us that Cade had put a move on her after the game—he had sidled up to her and grabbed her rump when no one was looking. She said she just gave him a look, and he backed off. She was laughing about it when she told us.

Beaterson drops his balled-up foil wrapper out his window into the parking lot of the fast-food place. He stuffs the last handful of fries into his mouth and throws the little white sack out the window. The wind takes it away until it dies in a puddle.

"You can get fined for that, you know," Summerfield says.

"What?"

"Littering. Not to mention it's just plain ugly."

"Don't even bother," Deshutsis says. "Don't waste your breath."

"It's terrible, though, it really is," Summerfield says to Beaterson. "How can you just throw your garbage out into the parking lot? To me, that's like vandalism. It really stinks."

"I'm doing a public service," Beaterson says.

"Yeah, right," Summerfield says.

"Do not pursue this," Deshutsis says to her. "Listen to me. You will regret it."

"Like I say, I'm performing a public service," Beaterson says.

"How do you figure that?" she says, ignoring Deshutsis's hand-waving.

"These fast-food joints," Beaterson says. "They hire high school students to work here. One of their main duties is to go out in the parking lot with a trash bag and pick up the litter. That's their job. They get paid to do it. I'm giving them employment. Job security. If it wasn't for people like me, there wouldn't be litter, so there wouldn't be any employment for these folks. They ought to thank me."

Summerfield shakes her head. "The irrationality of that argument is—is—"

"I told you, but would you listen to me?" Deshutsis says.

"I tell you what," Summerfield says. "I'll make you a deal. You go out there and pick up all your litter, and I won't play any smooth jazz for the rest of the drive to Astoria."

I can tell Beaterson's giving it some thought. Such is his hatred of smooth jazz. And such is Summerfield's deviousness. She pays attention to everything, and she's learning which of our buttons to push to get certain behaviors. She's always pleasant about it, but it scares me.

"I don't negotiate with terrorists," Beaterson finally says.

Good. I'd rather see him leave his garbage in the parking lot than see her win another one. She wins enough of them. Not all, but enough.

The other day, after one of our practices, we were at the cabana, playing pool. Tim Goon was there, too. In fact, Goon had just destroyed me at eight ball, so I had a while to wait for my turn to play again. I went down the hall to buy myself a can of pop from the vending machine. I put my coins in and made my selection. When I turned around, Summerfield was standing right there. I hadn't even heard her come up behind me, and I jumped.

"Got change for a five?" she said, looking into my eyes.

I nodded, and reached for my wallet. Maybe it was me, but she seemed to be standing a bit close. She was wearing shorts.

"So, Flint," she said. "What are you waiting for?"

"Huh?"

"How come you haven't called Malibu yet? She did give you her phone number a few days ago, right?"

Rachel said this in a friendly way, and maybe she just said it to show me that she'd been paying attention and was interested in my life. I just smiled and handed her five ones. I didn't say anything.

A car pulls in a few spaces away from us, and three cute girls get out and walk behind our car on their way to the entrance of the hamburger place. They're busy talking to each other, but their eyes notice us. One of the girls looks boldly at us without looking away, and there's a trace of a smile on her face.

We stare. Summerfield is saying something, but we're not listening. We're watching the girls.

"Hmm?" Deshutsis says.

"I was going to tell you about that movie I saw," Rachel says.

"Oh. Yeah. Go ahead," Deshutsis says. "Only remember what I warned you about the other day. No summaries of movie plots."

"I know, I know," she says. "But this was a great movie. It was Japanese with English subtitles, and it was the scariest movie I've seen since *The Exorcist.*"

She proceeds to tell us, in shot-by-shot detail, the entire plot of the movie. She is still telling it as she takes the on-ramp back onto I-5 southbound. We want to tell her to stop, but we don't. We have a long drive ahead of us. And we like the sound of her voice.

Still, enough is enough. I wait for a pause in her narrative, and then I jump in, take the plunge.

"So, Rachel," I say.

"Yeah?"

"What's with the legs?"